ENCOUNTERS
WITH
ENLIGHTENMENT

Saddhaloka

ENCOUNTERS WITH ENLIGHTENMENT

Stories from the Life of the Buddha

wisdom tree

First Published in the United Kingdom by
Windhorse Publications

First published 2008

Publisher's Note: Since this work is intended for a general readership, Pali and Sanskrit words have been transliterated without the diacritical marks that would have been appropriate in a work of a more scholarly nature.

ISBN 978-81-8328-126-3

Published by
Wisdom Tree
4779/23, Ansari Road
Darya Ganj, New Delhi-110 002
Ph.: 23247966/67/68

Printed in India

CONTENTS

About the Author

Saddhaloka was born David Luce in Jersey in 1948. He left the island to continue his education at Leeds University, where he obtained a BA in History and developed a strong interest in Eastern religions, especially Buddhism. After completing his degree he married and travelled overland to India, where he spent fourteen months visiting several of the holy places associated with the Buddha.

After returning to Britain he decided it was time to get 'down to earth' and spent the next five years working on farms, mostly as a herdsman. This included three years in Ireland in a village community with people with learning difficulties.

He maintained a strong interest in meditation and Buddhism, and in 1979 moved with his family to Norwich, where there were other Buddhists with young children. He was ordained within the Western Buddhist Order two years later and given the name Saddhaloka, which means 'light of faith'. He spent the next thirteen years working for the Norwich Buddhist Centre. As well as teaching meditation and Buddhism, he led courses in massage and communication skills.

In 1995 he moved to Padmaloka, a retreat centre in Norfolk, where he helps men to prepare for ordination. He also has a special interest in developing Buddhist activities in Finland, Estonia, and Russia. Saddhaloka now has three grown-up children and a grand-daughter.

INTRODUCTION

WHEN I WAS A TEENAGER, an uncle came to live with us in Jersey. He had spent much of his life in Burma and had expected to die there, but a new nationalist government had forced him to leave. When I started to develop an interest in Eastern religions, he gave me a book from his extensive library. It was *The Life of the Buddha*, a collection of stories and teachings from the Pali Canon, compiled by the English Buddhist monk, Nanamoli.

For ten years the book remained largely unopened. Then, a few months after I became seriously involved in Buddhism, I went on my first solitary retreat and decided to take it with me. During the two weeks of that retreat, the Buddha and the world of ancient India came vividly alive for me as never before. I gained a sense of the Buddha as a real human being, who ate and slept, and got sick and grew old as we all do, while communicating something quite extraordinary, not just in what he said, but also in such simple things as how he walked and ate and looked at people. In his disciples I recognized the same hopes and fears, struggles and disappointments, pettiness and great-heartedness, the same contradictions, that are to be found in his followers today. I have returned to *The Life of the Buddha* again and again, for in this book I found a doorway into the great treasury of the Pali Canon through which I could begin to explore the many volumes available in translation. Previously, these tomes had seemed rather daunting and inaccessible, but now their great store of riches had been opened up to me.

The Buddha lived in northern India two-and-a-half thousand years ago. After his Enlightenment, at the age of thirty-five, he spent the remaining forty-five years of his life wandering the roads and by-ways of the 'middle country', the area of northern India then dominated by the rival kingdoms of Magadha and Kosala. He taught anyone who was prepared to listen; kings and beggars, philosophers and farmers, housewives and courtesans, murderers and holy men. All these were among his disciples. The accounts of the Buddha's many meetings, along with summaries of his teachings, were memorized and recited by his monk disciples at their regular gatherings, and in this way they were passed down through the centuries. There were once many different collections of these stories and teachings, gathered together by various schools of the developing Buddhist tradition. As far as we know, only one complete collection has survived to the present day. It was written down in Sri Lanka about 500 years after the Buddha's death, and is known as the Pali Canon. This collection is now available in English in a number of translations, and details of some of these are given at the end of this book.

It is mostly from my reading within these translations over the past twenty years that this selection of stories is made. (There is very little about the early life of the Buddha-to-be in the Pali Canon, so in my account of his early years I have also drawn on a much later and more poetic text called the *Lalitavistara*.) There are many, many stories about the Buddha, and I have chosen those that have spoken to me and that in one way or another have moved me, whether to tears, to laughter, or to quiet reflection. Some of the stories encapsulate beautifully profound teachings of the Buddha, and provide a very good basis for study and contemplation. I have also included stories that capture different qualities of the Buddha: his wisdom, his reason and clarity, his mysteriousness, his practicality, his remarkable powers, his gentle humour, his courage and fearlessness, and, above all, his kindness and compassion.

I have retold the stories, rather than just collate different translations, because even in the best translations the idioms and Buddhist terms of the oral tradition can be a bit of an obstacle to the newcomer, and I wanted to make these stories accessible to as many people as possible. At the same time I have tried not to take advantage of my story-teller's licence and to be as true as possible to the mood and spirit of the original. For example, there was a beautiful formality in the way in which people addressed each other in ancient India, and I wanted to retain something of this rather than substitute an informality more suited to a modern idiom.

In reading these stories, we need to remember that those who originally recited them and listened to them did not live in the same sort of world as we do, and did not think as we do. Accounts of the Buddha's meetings with farmers and wandering holy men alternate quite naturally with tales of his meetings with gods (and there were many kinds of gods), yakshas (sometimes translated 'goblins' or 'fairies'), and maras (evil ones). I simply recount the stories of the Buddha's encounters with these strange and marvellous beings as they have been passed down, and leave it to you to arrive at your own interpretation.

At the end of each story is a verse from the *Dhammapada*, one of the oldest sections of the Pali Canon. Scholars have concluded that the collection of pithy and profound teachings that make up this scripture were 'set' in this form very early on. They therefore bring us very close to hearing the authentic voice of the Buddha. I have left these verses in the words of the translator, and added a few endnotes to elaborate on some terms with which the reader might not be familiar.

This book is not intended simply to be read from cover to cover, but as something to dip into again and again. My hope is that through these stories and the verses from the *Dhammapada*, the Buddha will begin to come alive for you as you travel with him in your imagination along the dusty roads of ancient India. More than that, I hope the book will encourage many people to go on to explore for themselves the great treasury of the Pali Canon, and discover within it the same inspiration and guidance that I am so grateful to have found there.

1

THE GOING FORTH

LONG AGO in ancient India, beneath the foothills of the Himalayas, there lived a fierce and proud warrior people called the Sakyans. They were rich and prosperous, and though neighbouring kings looked upon the Sakyan lands with envy, they left them to live in peace; it was obvious how terrible would be the cost of any attempt at conquest. The chosen king of the Sakyans was called Suddhodana, and he was loved by his people as a strong and just ruler. His wife, Queen Maya, was the daughter of a neighbouring king. At the time this story begins she was heavily pregnant with their first child and, as was the custom in those days, she set off for her father's kingdom so that the child could be born in her family home, with her mother and the womenfolk of the family to assist. She waited too long, however, before setting out from Kapilavatthu, the chief city of the Sakyans. It was a journey of some days, and while resting in a pleasant grove she went into labour. Out in the midst of the countryside, standing up and holding the branch of a tree, Queen Maya gave birth to a boy. A messenger sped back to Kapilavatthu with the joyful news that a son and heir was born to the king and queen.

With great happiness Suddhodana set out to meet his wife and son, but on his way he was met by another messenger with news that cast a cloud over his joy. Queen Maya had died, having known her son for just seven days. The baby prince was brought back to Kapilavatthu and named Siddhattha. He was given into the care of Maya's sister Pajapati, also a queen of Suddhodana, who had herself recently given birth.

A wise holy man called Asita, hearing of the birth, came to the palace, and Shuddhodana had the child brought to him. For a long time they stood together, and not a word was spoken. Then the old man made a prediction. The boy had a most auspicious future ahead of him, and two paths would open before him. He would either become a great, world-ruling king, or, disillusioned with wealth and power, he would give up everything to become an outstanding spiritual master and world teacher. Asita could not say which of these roads Siddhattha would follow, but the king, conscious and proud of his warrior lineage, was determined that it should be the path of kingship.

As he grew into manhood, Siddhattha learned the lore of his proud people. He learned to fight on horseback and from a chariot, to use a sword, a bow, and a spear. He grew strong, courageous, and handsome, and became loved by all. He knew that he was born to be a leader of his people, and to enjoy the power and privilege of kingship, as well as how to bear its responsibilities.

Bearing in mind the prediction of Asita, Suddhodana did all he could to ensure that Siddhattha enjoyed the sweetest pleasures of worldly life. He dwelt in beautiful palaces, with ponds and sweet-scented flowers, fine musicians, dancing girls, and youthful servants. When the time came for him to marry, a beautiful princess called Yasodhara was chosen to be his wife, and in time a son was born whom they named Rahula. It seemed that Siddhattha's cup was full and that he had the best that life could offer. Yet now, when his life should have been full of happiness, a strange and restless mood of unease and discontent began to afflict the prince. He tried to throw it off, but the pleasures he was accustomed to seemed hollow and unfulfilling, and their failure to make him happy served to increase his discontent. Sensing that something was amiss, Suddhodana sought to distract the prince with new kinds of entertainments and diversions, but to no avail.

One day, feeling restless, and burdened by the life of the palace, Siddhattha summoned his charioteer Channa to harness up a chariot and horses. Together they galloped out through the city, and as they sped along Siddhattha began to feel his oppressive mood lift. Suddenly he saw something that made him grab Channa's arm and shout at him to stop. As the chariot came to a halt the prince pointed to a bent figure shuffling along by the side of the road.

'Look Channa, look there! What is that? What is that?' he demanded.

'What, him?' Channa was bemused, and at the same time concerned at seeing Siddhattha so pale and shaken. 'Why that's just an old man. He's lost his hair and teeth. His skin is wrinkled, his body is bent and worn. The years go by and that's what happens. It's just an old man. What's wrong, my prince?'

'Will I be an old man, Channa? Will my son Rahula be an old man? Will Yasodhara grow old like that?'

'We all grow old, my prince. King or beggar, there is no way round it I'm afraid. We all grow old.'

Siddhattha fell silent, shaken to the core of his being. As if for the first time, he saw the inevitability of old age and the suffering that comes with it, and this cruel fact of life burned itself deep into his being. Never again would he see things through the eyes of innocent youth. Sobered and deep in thought, he waved Channa to take him back to the palace.

A few days later Siddhattha and Channa rode out again. They had not driven far when again Siddhattha shouted at Channa to stop. His eyes had fallen on a figure lying by the roadside writhing in agony and lost in a delirium of pain, oblivious to those who tried to soothe him.

'Channa!' he cried 'What is happening? What is wrong with that man?'

'That man is ill, my prince. He is in pain. It happens. Such is life!'

This time it was the fact of sickness, that could at any moment snatch away health and happiness, that had seared itself into Siddhattha's consciousness, and he saw as never before the frailty of human life. Again he returned to the palace shaken and pondering deeply on what he had seen.

Not many days had passed before Siddhattha again summoned Channa to prepare the chariot. As they rode along, they came to a crossroads where Channa stopped as four men passed in front of them carrying a stretcher on their shoulders. On the stretcher lay a motionless figure wrapped in white cloth, his face painted white, flowers heaped on his chest. It was a funeral procession, and the men of the family were carrying a relative's body down to the cremation ground by the river to be burned. The prince now found himself confronting the fact of death. As if for the first time, he recognized its awful inevitability. As sure as we are born, so we must die. 'But how can one make any sense of a life so soon overtaken by old age, always vulnerable to sickness, and bound to end in death?' he asked himself. 'How can one find any happiness, any pleasure, in such a life?'

This great question seemed to take over Siddhattha, so that he became distant even from those closest to him, and little interested in food or the other pleasures and activities of his daily life. Somewhere deep within he sensed there must be an answer, a key to this mystery, and that he must do everything in his power to find it.

Restless and preoccupied, Siddhattha went out once again with Channa. As they rode along in the chariot, the prince's eyes now fell on a fourth sight. Walking by the side of the road he saw a wandering holy man, clad in a ragged robe, carrying a staff and begging-bowl, calm, serene, and self-contained. A strange peace descended on Siddhattha, and as he gazed on this homeless seeker after truth he knew what he himself had to do. He would give up wealth, family, and power, and himself go forth as a homeless wanderer. There was no alternative. For his own good, for the sake of those he loved, for the benefit of all, he would give himself completely, utterly, to the search for the truth that would bring freedom from old age, sickness, and death.

When Siddhattha told his father of his resolve, the old king would have none of it. He remembered Asita's prediction and foresaw his worst fears being realized. He tried reason and persuasion. He appealed to Siddhattha's sense of duty. He offered him powers and responsibilities, anything he thought might tempt his son to stay. As a final precaution he had extra guards posted around the palace. But Siddhattha was not to be swayed from his purpose.

So it was that, a few days later, at dead of night, Siddhattha stood and looked on his sleeping wife and child, afraid to give them even a farewell kiss in case he woke them. They looked so beautiful, so peaceful. Recollecting his great resolve, he turned away from them with an aching heart and slipped out of the palace to where the faithful Channa was waiting with his horse. He mounted, and Channa ran beside him as they journeyed through the night and into the dawn to the river that marked the edge of the Sakyan territory. Here they rested, and Siddhattha prepared himself for the step he was about to take. He slowly removed his jewels and finery, and cut off his long hair with his sword. A hunter passed by, dressed in the clothes of a wandering holy man, and the prince called him over and asked him to exchange the saffron robes he was wearing for the royal silks. The hunter could not believe his luck. The deal was quickly done and Siddhattha wrapped himself in the pieces of coarse cloth. He cut himself a rough wooden staff and picked up the alms bowl he would use to beg for food. Exchanging fond farewells with Channa, he gave him a message to take back to his father. Then the former prince walked down to the river and began to wade across it. Setting his face determinedly towards his new life, Siddhattha did not once look back over his shoulder towards his home and all he had left behind.

What mirth can there be, what pleasure, when all the time (everything) is blazing (with the threefold fire of suffering, impermanence, and insubstantiality)? Covered (though you are) in blind darkness, you do not seek a light!

Dhammapada 146

2

THE WANDERER

THUS SIDDHATTHA THE PRINCE became Gotama the wandering holy man, now known simply by the name of his family. He had been used to the luxury of palace life, and at first he found life as a wanderer very difficult. He had always eaten the finest food, delicacies prepared by accomplished chefs and served in elegant dishes. Now he begged his first meal from poor villagers and went to sit under a tree outside the village to eat it. When he looked at the poor country food all mixed up together in his wooden bowl, he retched and vomited, but he persisted, and such was his determination that he soon felt at home in this simple, hard life, and able to turn his mind to his great purpose.

Gotama had set out in search of truth, but where was he to look? He soon found he was not alone in his searching. He had been born during a time of great spiritual ferment in India, and there were many wandering holy men like him. They lived outside the normal boundaries of society, homeless and owning nothing, but much respected and readily supported by rich and poor alike. It occurred to him that one among them might have already found what he was looking for. He decided to seek out the greatest teachers of his day.

He went first to a teacher called Alara Kalama, who taught as the highest truth the realization of a state he called 'no-thingness'. Gotama became his disciple and followed his instructions with single-mindedness and devotion. Very soon he had realized for himself this state of 'no-thingness'. While dwelling in this deep meditative state, he experienced great bliss and peace, but when he returned to everyday consciousness, he found to his disappointment and consternation that the great problems of old age, sickness, and death remained. He asked Alara Kalama to teach him more, but the old sage had no more to teach. Recognizing that in Gotama he had an exceptional student, Alara Kalama offered to share with him the leadership of all his disciples and his reputation as one of the greatest spiritual masters of his day. Gotama, however, despite feeling great respect and gratitude towards his first teacher, could not rest content with any lesser goal than the overcoming of old age, sickness, and death that had driven him to go forth in the first place, so he bade him farewell and journeyed on.

There was only one other teacher with a reputation equal to that of Alara Kalama. He was called Uddaka Ramaputta, and he taught that the highest realization was to be found in a state he called 'neither-perception-nor-non-perception'. Gotama sought him out and asked him to teach him all he knew. Again with great determination and application Gotama quickly realized this goal for himself, but again he remained dissatisfied. Immersed in beautiful and refined states of meditation he might forget about old age, sickness, and death, but as soon as he emerged from meditation the great question of how to make sense of this life reasserted itself with a vengeance. Like Alara Kalama, Uddaka Ramaputta recognized the rare spiritual qualities in his disciple, and offered to hand over to Gotama the leadership of his disciples. Again, knowing this would be a dead end, Gotama declined and moved on.

Barely a year had passed since he first left home, and already Gotama had trained under the greatest teachers of his day, and found them lacking. There was no one else to learn from. What was he to do next?

Among his fellow wanderers there were many who followed the path of asceticism. They believed that if one could completely crush all sense desires and subjugate the body, and at the same time completely control the mind, a higher consciousness would eventually fly free, and the mystery of life would be solved. Their methods involved a huge variety of extreme austerities. Gotama resolved to follow this path, and took it up with a fierce determination. He sought out the most lonely and awesome places, including those inhabited by ghosts and wild animals, and when fear and terror came over him he stood firm, refusing to give way to them. Whatever he was doing when the fear arose, he continued to do until it had subsided; if he was sitting, he remained sitting, if he was walking, he remained walking, if he was lying down, he remained lying down. In this way he gradually overcame his fear and dread.

He practised breath control exercises that led him to feel as if violent winds filled his head, or as if someone was splitting his head with a sword, or tightening a rough leather strap around his head. At times it felt as though a butcher was carving up his stomach, or he was being roasted over hot coals. Tenaciously he applied himself, and though he became mentally and physically exhausted, he never allowed the painful feelings that arose to gain any hold over his mind. He ate less and less, and became gaunt and emaciated. His limbs looked like bamboos, his backside 'like a camel's hoof'. His ribs stuck out like the rafters of a ruined barn and his eyes were sunk deep in their sockets, so that to look into them was like looking into a deep well for the gleam of water at the bottom. When he touched his belly he felt his backbone, and when he rubbed his skin the hair fell away, rotted at its roots.

For over five years Gotama pursued this path of asceticism, with an unflinching resolve that aroused awe and admiration in all who came across him. His fame spread as he pushed himself further than any ascetic before him had had the courage or strength of mind to do. Five close disciples followed him everywhere, waiting for him to finally break through.

Then, one day, while bathing in a river, Gotama fell over and found he was in such an enfeebled state that he could barely lift himself up again. This narrow escape from drowning made him realize that if he continued much longer he would soon be dead, and no closer to his goal.

He was going down a blind alley. Upon this realization, he abandoned this path of harsh asceticism, took simple nutritious food, and began to feel his strength return. Seeing him eating such food, his five followers deserted him in disgust, convinced he had betrayed them by returning to a life of luxury. Unperturbed, Gotama pondered deeply on what he should do next.

Suddenly, there came to him a memory from his childhood. He recalled how, sitting in the shade of a rose-apple tree one spring, watching his father at work in a field as he ploughed the ceremonial first furrow, an experience of spontaneous peace, bliss, and happiness had flooded over him and absorbed him for many hours. In that experience he sensed a new way forward.

One who does not make use of his (spiritual) opportunities, who, though young and strong, is lazy, weak in aspiration, and inactive, such a lazy person does not find the way to understanding.

Dhammapada 280

3

ENLIGHTENMENT

THE HARSH AUSTERITIES of the previous five years were all abandoned. Begging simple nutritious food, Gotama slowly built up his strength and restored his health, and as he travelled he came to a cool and pleasant grove of trees near the River Neranjara. It was far enough from fields or a village for him to know he would not be disturbed, yet close enough to habitation for him to be able to beg the daily meal with which he sustained himself. He decided to stay there and to begin to explore the new vistas opened up by the memory of his blissful boyhood experience beneath the rose-apple tree. As the summer heat built up he devoted himself to meditation. New depths of his mind and being began to open up to him. Finally, on a beautiful full-moon night, sensing that at last his time had come, Gotama settled himself beneath a spreading peepul tree on a pile of kusa grass given him by a cowherd. He vowed that even though his flesh might wither and his blood dry up, he would not rise from that spot until he had attained his goal. He entered into ever deeper, clearer, more peaceful meditation, never allowing himself to become intoxicated by the pleasurable and joyful feelings that flooded through him, nor letting them gain any power over his mind.

He saw countless past lives unfold before him, life after life after life. He saw universes arising and dissolving. He saw how beings were born and passed away according to their actions; good and skilful actions leading to a happy rebirth, bad and unskilful ones to a painful rebirth. He saw into the very heart of existence, and understood how suffering grew from craving and ignorance, and how – with minds rooted in craving, hatred, and delusion – beings launched themselves again and again into an endless round of birth, sickness, old age, and death. Perceiving all this, and seeing through it, his heart was finally set free. A profound turning about took place in the depths of his being. He had become a Buddha, an Enlightened One, one who knows.

For several weeks the newly-awakened Buddha hardly left the grove of trees. He sat and absorbed the immensity and wonder of his new vision and understanding. Then, slowly, he began to turn his mind towards the world and to how he might share with others the peace and wisdom he had found. He thought, 'This truth I have discovered is so subtle and so profound. It goes far beyond anything that can be put into words. If I try to teach it to others they will only misunderstand. That will surely be painful for them and painful for me.' This thought of the Buddha's was immediately apparent to all the gods in all the heavens.

They had been watching his progress with great satisfaction and there had been much rejoicing among them when he finally attained his goal. But when they saw him hesitate they were filled with concern and apprehension.

'A Buddha has finally arisen in the world,' they said to one another. 'The way to freedom is opened up. But what will become of the world, what will become of all beings, if he does not teach?'

At that very instant, Brahma Sahampati, king of all the gods, appeared before the Buddha in the form of a beautiful golden youth. He entreated the Buddha to teach the spiritual path for the sake of those who would be able to understand. There were surely some beings who had only a little dust on their eyes and who were thirsting for the truth that he had discovered.

The Buddha looked out over the world, and with his Enlightened vision he saw its countless beings as lotuses in a pond. Some remained sunk deep in the stinking mud at the bottom of the pond, ignorant and unheeding, while others were beginning to rise up through the clarifying waters towards the light. Others stood clear of the water, needing just a little sunshine to coax them out of their buds. Great compassion, inseparable from the wisdom of a Buddha, blazed in his heart. For the sake of those who would be able to hear and understand, he resolved to find a way to express his experience of Enlightenment and to teach others how to attain it.

Many a birth have I undergone in this (process of) faring on (in the round of conditioned existence), seeking the builder of the house and not finding him. Painful is (such) repeated birth.

House-builder, (now) you are seen! Never again shall you build (me) a house. Your rafters are all broken, your ridgepole shattered. The (conditioned) mind too has gone to destruction: one has attained to the cessation of craving.

Dhammapada 153–4

4

THE FIRST DISCIPLES

THE TIME HAD COME for the Buddha to set out from the peaceful grove where he had finally found the truth he had long sought, and to begin to share it with others.

'Who shall I teach first?' he asked himself. 'Who will be able to understand this great truth that is so profound and so subtle?' The Buddha's thoughts turned to his own teachers, Alara Kalama and Uddaka Ramaputta, with whom he had trained at the very start of his quest. They were sincere and gifted men who would surely understand, but with his divine eye he saw that both had recently died.

Next, he thought of the five wanderers who had been his disciples during the time of his great austerities, and who had abandoned him when he began to take food again. Once again using his divine eye, he saw they were in the Deer Park at Isipatana (Sarnath), and he set out to find them.

It was the season of hot sun and torrential monsoon rains, and the journey from the grove by the Neranjara to Isipatana covered many miles. After travelling on foot for many days the Buddha came at last to Isipatana and to the Deer Park. The five ascetics, his former disciples, were sitting together under a tree when they saw a figure in the robes of a holy man approaching in the distance. He seemed familiar, and they soon realized who it was. 'It is that wanderer Gotama who betrayed us, who gave up the struggle and returned to a life of luxury! What does he want here?' they said among themselves.

They decided to ignore him, to pay him none of the respect they had shown him when they had revered him as the greatest of all ascetics. As the Buddha came closer, however, they found themselves unable to adhere to their resolution. Something in his manner and bearing commanded their respect, and they rose to greet him as they would an honoured guest. One of them took his robe and bowl, another prepared a seat of folded robes, and a third fetched water to wash his feet.

At first, the atmosphere between them was awkward and uncomfortable. The five ascetics still felt betrayed by Gotama, and they could not imagine how anyone who had abandoned the spiritual path as they understood it could possibly have gained the wisdom they all sought. Yet they had to admit that the figure now before them was not the Gotama they had known. It was not simply that he was restored to health, and no longer the drawn and emaciated ascetic they had lived with. Even though tired and dusty after his long journey, he shone with a peculiar radiance and beauty. It felt strange and remarkable to be in his presence, even just sitting in silence with him. When he spoke, his words seemed to come from great depths of wisdom and understanding. He communicated with kindness and compassion such as they had never before encountered. The five were soon won over and they willingly opened their hearts to the Buddha.

As he talked to them, the immensity and significance of what was happening slowly dawned on the five ascetics, and to start with it seemed almost too much for them to comprehend. Yes, Gotama had indeed conquered old age, sickness, and death! He really did know! He had discovered the truth in search of which they, like him, had given up everything. He had attained what they had spent so many long and difficult years struggling to attain. And now here he was, sitting with them, and sharing with them this new-found truth. It was all they had dreamed of, all they had longed for. A mood of great excitement, urgency, and earnestness was born.

As they sat together beneath the tree in the Deer Park, the Buddha began to teach. He sought to give old words new meaning and significance, to push these wanderers beyond the limits of their present experience into a new vision of existence. Sometimes the Buddha taught, sometimes they asked him questions, sometimes they just sat in silence together, reflecting and meditating. There seemed little time for sleep or food. To sustain themselves, the five ascetics would take it in turns to go in pairs and beg enough food to share between them all. Day passed into night, and night into day. Suddenly, a smile lit the face of Kondanna, one of the five. He and the Buddha looked at each other, and there was an immediate sense of joyful recognition.

'Kondanna knows! Kondanna knows!' the Buddha exclaimed. The truth had been communicated, and there was now a second Enlightened being in the world. Over the following days, one by one, the other wanderers came also to understand, and to share, the wisdom and compassion of the Buddha. Thus they were six.

Many people, out of fear, flee for refuge to (sacred) hills, woods, groves, trees, and shrines.

In reality this is not a safe refuge. In reality this is not the best refuge. Fleeing to such a refuge one is not released from all suffering.

He who goes for refuge to the Enlightened One, to the Truth, and to the Spiritual Community, and who sees with perfect wisdom the Four Ariyan Truths –

namely, suffering, the origin of suffering, the passing beyond suffering, and the Ariyan Eight-membered Way leading to the pacification of suffering –

(for him) this is a safe refuge, (for him) this is the best refuge. Having gone to such a refuge one is released from all suffering.

Dhammapada 188–92

5

THE COMMUNITY GROWS

NOT LONG AFTER the Enlightenment of the five ascetics the Buddha was seated alone beneath a tree in the Deer Park at Isipatana, having spent the night in meditation. Towards dawn he saw coming towards him, through the mist, a young nobleman, dressed in all his finery, wearing slippers woven in gold thread. This young man was obviously very downcast and distressed, and was repeating to himself, 'It is frightening, it is horrible.' This young man was called Yasa, and he was the son of a rich merchant who lived in Baranasi. Waking very early after a night of music and merry-making, he had looked around the room at the attendants and dancing-girls. The night before, they had seemed so alluring, but now they lay arms and bodies all akimbo, some of them snoring, some dribbling, others grunting in their sleep. A feeling of revulsion at the emptiness of the life he was leading engulfed him. He walked out of the palace, and was wandering aimlessly and anxiously in the woods when he came across the Buddha.

The Buddha signalled Yasa to join him. 'Come Yasa, and I will teach you the truth,' the Buddha said. 'Here is something that is not frightening and not horrible.' As he heard these words from the serene and beautiful stranger, a sense of joy and hope immediately replaced the despondent mood into which Yasa had fallen. He kicked off his golden slippers, sat down eagerly next to the holy man, and listened intently to what he had to say. The Buddha led him progressively deeper towards the truth, so that as he sat there 'knowledge and vision of things as they really are' arose in Yasa.

Back at the palace, Yasa's mother had awoken to find her son missing and went in great distress to her husband. Servants were sent to search for the youth. Yasa's father joined the search, and set off into the Deer Park.

While he was still some distance from the spot where the Buddha and Yasa were sitting silently together, the Buddha saw Yasa's father coming. Knowing who he was, he used his mental powers to prevent the rich merchant from seeing his son. As he came close to the Buddha, Yasa's father immediately recognized the golden slippers lying nearby. He described his son to the holy man, and asked if he had seen such a youth. The Buddha replied that indeed he had, and invited the merchant to sit with him, with the promise that he would soon see Yasa. Greatly relieved, the merchant sat down, and was soon deep in conversation with the Buddha. As the hours passed the Buddha taught him, and eventually he too gained insight into the truth of things. Delighted and grateful he asked to be accepted as a disciple, and dedicated his life to his new teacher.

While the Buddha and the merchant were speaking together, Yasa remained immersed in deep meditation, and attained full Enlightenment. Knowing what had happened, the Buddha allowed the merchant to see his son. Yasa's father was overjoyed, and urged the young man to return with him to their palace to set his mother's mind at rest. The newly Enlightened Yasa gave the Buddha a meaningful look, and aware of his thoughts the Buddha turned to the merchant and asked him a question. 'Do you think, good sir, that one who has fully realized the truth could ever really return to the householder's life?' The merchant acknowledged that this would not be possible. The Buddha then told him that Yasa had that very morning joined the company of the Enlightened Ones. With great emotion the merchant realized his son would never return with him to their palatial home, but remain with the Buddha. His life would never be the same. Accepting this with feelings of both joy and sadness, the merchant invited the Buddha and his followers, including Yasa, to a meal later that day. The Buddha agreed, and the merchant returned home to break the news to his family and to prepare for his guests. A fine meal was laid on, after which the Buddha taught Yasa's mother and his former wife, and they also became his disciples.

Yasa was a lively and fun-loving young man, very popular with the people of the area. When word got round that he had become a monk, his friends and acquaintances became very curious and were keen to meet the Buddha. 'There must be something quite extraordinary about this teacher,' they said to one another, 'if he can win over even our Yasa.' One by one they came, and each in turn was deeply affected by his meeting with the Buddha. Within a few days not only Yasa, but also many of his friends, had become disciples of the Buddha and gone forth as homeless wanderers.

Word spread, and day after day people flocked to see the Buddha and hear him teach. Many devoted themselves to him, to his teachings, and to the community of his followers. The Buddha radiated a tremendous positive energy. and among these earliest disciples there was an intense sense of urgency and a vibrant feeling of anything being possible. Many of them became Enlightened within a very short space of time, and soon the six had grown to seven, to eleven, to sixty-one.

One day, the Buddha gathered together all these disciples and exhorted them to go out into the world to wander from place to place. He told them to teach the way to Enlightenment for the welfare and the happiness of the many, out of compassion for the world. With this exhortation ringing in their ears they parted, spread out in all directions, and took the Buddha's message into the towns and villages of ancient India. The Buddha also set off alone to wander and to teach.

'All conditioned things are impermanent.' When one sees this with insight one becomes weary of suffering. This is the Way to Purity.

'All conditioned things are painful.' When one sees this with insight one becomes weary of suffering. This is the Way to Purity.

'All things (whatsoever) are devoid of unchanging selfhood.' When one sees this with insight one becomes weary of suffering. This is the Way to Purity.

Dhammapada 277–9

6

THE FIRE WORSHIPPERS

DURING HIS WANDERINGS, the Buddha came to a place called Uruvela, where there lived a thousand fire-worshipping ascetics who wore their hair in long matted dreadlocks. They were led by three holy men who all went by the name of Kassapa. Kassapa of Uruvela had 500 disciples, Kassapa of the River had 300, and Kassapa of Gaya had 200.

The Buddha went to the hermitage of Kassapa of Uruvela and asked to spend the night in the fire chamber where the ascetic performed his ritual worship. Kassapa had no objection, but warned the Buddha that a terrible naga, a dragon-like serpent, lived in the chamber. It was immensely powerful and deadly venomous, and it would almost certainly kill him. The Buddha seemed quite happy to risk his life in this way, so a slightly bemused Kassapa agreed to let him stay in the fire chamber.

The Buddha entered the chamber, put down a reed mat, and sat down to meditate. When the dragon-serpent saw this he became very angry and poured smoke into the room, intending to drive out the intruder, but the Buddha responded by producing even more smoke. At this, the naga flew into a rage and produced flames, but the Buddha retaliated with flames of his own, so that the fire chamber seemed to glow like a great furnace. 'Well, that's the end of that monk!' thought Kassapa smugly, as he looked on, but in the morning, to Kassapa's surprise, the Buddha emerged unscathed from the fire chamber and presented the serpent to him, now just a little snake coiled up harmlessly in his begging-bowl. Kassapa was grudgingly impressed, but he believed himself superior to the Buddha, and said to himself, 'This monk is indeed powerful, but he's not an Enlightened master like me!'

The following evening, the Buddha went to stay in a nearby forest, and during the night the four great kings, the protectors of the world, came to pay homage to him and hear him teach. As the Buddha taught, a great light illuminated the forest and the sky so that it could be seen from all around. In the morning, Kassapa, who had seen this magical occurrence, asked the Buddha who had visited him during the night. When the Buddha told him that the four divine kings had come to hear him teach, he was greatly impressed, but reassured himself thinking, 'This monk is indeed powerful, but he is not an Enlightened master like me!'

Soon after this, Kassapa's great fire ceremony fell due, to which people from many miles around would come, bringing food and other fine offerings. Kassapa thought to himself, not without a little anxiety, 'Many of my devotees will be coming tomorrow, and if that monk Gotama performs one of his marvels in front of them, his reputation will grow and mine will decline. I really hope he doesn't come.' Knowing Kassapa's thoughts, the Buddha took himself off, and was not present for the fire ceremony. The following day, hiding his relief and pretending disappointment, Kassapa enquired as to where the Buddha had been. The Buddha told Kassapa quite straightforwardly how he had read his thoughts and, knowing his fears, had journeyed far away. Kassapa was a little discomfited, but nevertheless he thought once again to himself, 'This monk is indeed powerful, but he is not an Enlightened master like me!'

As the days passed, things continued in this manner, the Buddha displaying again and again his remarkable powers, and the conceited Kassapa continuing to think to himself, 'He is not an Enlightened master like me!'

Wishing to help him see the truth of things, the Buddha eventually decided that a sharp shock was needed. He said bluntly to Kassapa, 'Listen, Kassapa, you are not an Enlightened master, nor are you on the way to becoming one. Furthermore, nothing you are doing will enable you to become one, or even to enter the path to Enlightenment. Do you understand?'

With this sharp jolt, Kassapa's self-deception finally crumbled, and he recognized the vast difference between himself and the Buddha. He threw himself humbly at the Buddha's feet and asked to be accepted as his disciple. The Buddha was happy to receive him, but Kassapa had a large following of disciples who believed in him and whom it would not be right for him to abandon without consultation. Therefore, before he would accept Kassapa as a disciple, the Buddha insisted that he explain his intentions to his disciples and free them from their obligation to him, so that they could choose their own path. Having witnessed the recent events, and seen for themselves the Buddha's powers, every one of Kassapa's followers chose to join him as a disciple of the Buddha. They cut off their matted dreadlocks and threw them into the river, along with their ritual implements, and dedicated themselves to the Buddha and his teaching.

Further down the river, Kassapa of the River and his followers saw all the dreadlocks and ritual implements floating past, and wondered what on earth was going on. They became very worried what might have happened to Kassapa of Uruvela and his disciples, and they set off up river to find out.

When they discovered what had happened, Kassapa of the River asked Kassapa of Uruvela, 'Is this path better?' 'It most certainly is!' came the reply. So Kassapa of the River consulted his 300 disciples, who all decided to become followers of the Buddha. Soon, another 300 sets of matted dreadlocks and ritual implements were floating down the river.

These were spotted by Kassapa of Gaya and his 200 followers. They in turn became anxious as to the fate of their fellow fire-worshippers, and they hastened to Uruvela to find out what had happened. Soon, they too were convinced of the superiority of the Buddha's teaching and became his disciples. Thus the community of his followers grew by 1,000.

If month after month for a hundred years one should offer sacrifices by the thousand, and if for a single moment one should venerate a (spiritually) developed person, better is that (act of) veneration than the hundred years (of sacrifices).

Though a man should tend the sacred fire in the forest for a hundred years, yet if he venerates a (spiritually) developed person even for a moment, better is that (act of) veneration than the hundred years (spent tending the sacred fire).

Dhammapada 106–7

7

NANDA AND THE NYMPHS

SEVEN YEARS had passed since the morning when Prince Siddhattha had exchanged his silks and jewels for the robes of a wanderer and waded across the river that marked the boundary of the Sakyan territory, leaving his former life behind forever. Now Enlightened, Gotama returned to the land of the Sakyans. Though it was only one year after his Enlightenment, his fame as a great holy man and teacher was spreading quickly throughout northern India. The Sakyans, however, were a proud race, and they were at first reluctant to show any respect to this man whom they felt had spurned them and their warrior tradition when he left to become a monk. It was especially difficult for the old king, Suddhodana, who had keenly felt the loss of his son, and whom the intervening years had greatly aged. Now he felt a mixture of great joy at seeing his son again, and intense sadness at seeing him clad in the ragged robes of a wandering holy man. It pained him above all to think that his son, a Sakyan prince, was going from door to door begging his food from the people who should have been his subjects. Suddhodana tried to dissuade his son, saying it was not befitting for one of his lineage to be begging food on the streets of Kapilavatthu. Gotama replied that his lineage was now that of the Buddhas, and that it had always been their tradition to live without home or possessions, and to beg for their food, so he would continue to do so. Nevertheless, he agreed that he and his followers would from time to time receive a ceremonial meal as guests of one family or another.

Suddhodana lost no time in inviting them to his palace, on a day coinciding with a celebration to mark the forthcoming marriage of the Buddha's half-brother, Nanda, to a beautiful Sakyan noblewoman. The two men sat side by side at the meal, and as the Buddha got up to leave he handed Nanda his begging-bowl. Nanda did not know quite what to do, but out of respect and good manners he followed the Buddha, carrying his bowl, out of the palace and all the way back to the grove outside the city where the Buddha and his followers were staying. As Nanda left the room with the Buddha, his bride-to-be called to him, 'Come back soon, Prince,' but it proved to be a long time before she saw him again. When they arrived at the grove, the Buddha asked Nanda if he would not like to give up the household life and follow him. It had all happened rather quickly, and Nanda was confused. He did not have any great inclination towards the spiritual life, but had a great deal of respect for his half-brother, and because of this he agreed, and was immediately ordained as a monk.

Some time later, after they had left Kapilavatthu, some of the other disciples came to the Buddha to tell him that Nanda, though now a monk, was still holding to the ways of the palace, wearing robes that had been carefully pressed and ironed, putting oil on his eyes, and using a fine glazed bowl. The Buddha called Nanda to him and asked him if what he had heard was true. When Nanda admitted that it was, the Buddha took him to task, pointing out that having given up everything for the spiritual life, he should now be living in the forest, eating food got by begging, wearing robes made of rags collected on refuse-heaps, and having nothing to do with the desires of the senses. Nanda was humbled, and tried to mend his ways, but he could still not completely reconcile himself to this hard, simple life.

About two years after he had left the palace to follow the Buddha, Nanda came very close to giving up the spiritual life altogether. He began telling other monks of his dissatisfaction with the monastic lifestyle and of his yearning for the world he had left behind in Kapilavatthu. Again, word of this got back to the Buddha. He called Nanda and asked him if it was true that he was thinking of giving up the holy life.

'It is Lord.'

'But why, Nanda?'

'When I left with you that day, the beautiful Sakyan girl who was to be my wife looked at me and said, "Come back soon, Prince." Again and again I think of her, and I am not happy living this life.'

At this, the Buddha took Nanda by the arm and in an instant took him to a heavenly world, where they saw 500 exquisitely beautiful dancing nymphs, with delicate pink feet.

'Do you see those 500 nymphs, Nanda?'

'Yes, Lord, I certainly do!'

'So tell me, Nanda. Which is more beautiful, more attractive; your Sakyan girl, or these 500 nymphs.'

Nanda did not have any doubt. Compared to these nymphs his Sakyan beauty was like a monkey with its nose and ears cut off.

'Then enjoy the holy life, Nanda, and I will guarantee you will have 500 nymphs just like these!'

'If the Buddha can guarantee me 500 nymphs like these, I shall certainly enjoy the holy life.'

Nanda threw himself into his spiritual life with renewed zest and enthusiasm, and did not hide the source of his inspiration. It was not long before news spread among the other disciples that the monk Nanda was following the holy life for the sake of nymphs. His former friends became scornful of him and would have nothing to do with him. He was shocked, and then ashamed and humiliated by their scornful comments. He went alone into the forest and applied himself to meditation as never before, pursuing the goal of the spiritual life with unprecedented determination and energy. His wholehearted efforts bore fruit, and before the sun rose he gained Enlightenment and shared fully in the wisdom and compassion of the Buddhas.

Having returned from the forest the next day, Nanda went to see the Buddha.

'Lord, about those 500 nymphs you promised me. I release you from that promise.'

The Buddha smiled. 'I know it, Nanda,' he replied. 'The moment your heart was freed of all craving, I was also freed from my promise.'

Those who have not led the spiritual life, or obtained the wealth (of merit) in their youth, (such as these) brood over the past like aged herons in a pond without fish.

Those who have not led the spiritual life, or obtained the wealth (of merit) in their youth, (such as these) lie like worn-out arrows, lamenting the things of old.

Dhammapada 155–6

8

RAHULA

WHEN PRINCE SIDDHATTHA had set out on his quest, the son he'd left behind had been just a baby. By the time the Buddha returned to visit Kapilavatthu, Prince Rahula was seven years old. Gotama and his large extended family were soon on warm terms again, though on a very different basis from in the past, and the Buddha was soon a regular visitor at the palace. During one of these visits, Yasodhara, his former wife, sent the boy to the Buddha, telling him to ask his father for his inheritance, hoping that perhaps he would formally make over all his rights to his son. The young prince followed the Buddha around saying, 'Give me my inheritance, monk. Give me my inheritance, monk.' The Buddha, however, chose not to understand this request in the way that Yasodhara had intended it. He had already explained to King Suddhodana that he now considered himself to be of no earthly royal lineage, but of the noble lineage of the Buddhas. If he had any inheritance to pass on, it was his wisdom and compassion, which were the true birthright of any human being prepared to make the effort to attain them. So as the boy continued to follow him around, persisting in his request, the Buddha told Sariputta, one of his chief disciples, to ordain him. In this way Rahula became a boy monk, enjoying Sariputta's care and tutelage.

When he heard of this, the old king was very upset. As he saw it, he had now lost not only his son, but also his grandson, both heirs to his title and riches. Seeing his distress, the Buddha agreed that in the future no boy would be ordained without the permission of his parents, but Rahula remained a monk, and when the time came for the Buddha and his followers to leave Kapilavatthu he went with them. Gotama took a close personal interest in Rahula's progress, frequently spending time teaching the young monk.

Four years after leaving Kapilavatthu, the Buddha sat with the eleven-year-old Rahula to teach him about morality. He took a ladle and poured into it a small amount of water.

'Rahula, do you see this little bit of water in the ladle?'

'Yes Lord.'

'Well, if people are not careful to avoid deliberately telling lies, there is as little good in them as this.'

The Buddha then threw away the water and asked Rahula if he had seen what he had done.

'Yes Lord.'

'Rahula, unless people are careful to avoid deliberately telling lies they throw away the good in them just like that.'

Turning the ladle upside-down the Buddha said, 'Rahula, unless people are careful to avoid deliberately telling lies, they treat the good in themselves like this.'

Turning the ladle the right way up again, the Buddha asked, 'Rahula, do you see how this ladle is now quite empty?'

'Yes Lord.'

'Unless people are careful to avoid deliberately telling lies they are empty of goodness, just like this ladle. Imagine a great royal war elephant. If in battle that elephant used his head and tusks and legs and body, but kept back his trunk, then that royal elephant is not yet fully trained. Only when he also uses his trunk is he fully trained. In the same way, until someone is always careful to avoid deliberately lying, I do not consider them fully trained. You must train yourself, Rahula, never to tell a lie, even as a joke. What is a mirror for, Rahula?'

'For looking at oneself, Lord.'

'You must always be looking at yourself, Rahula, examining all your acts of body, speech, and mind.'

In ways such as this the Buddha taught Rahula while he was a boy, and as he grew into a youth and a young man. When he was twenty-one, Rahula gained Enlightenment.

Though one should conquer in battle thousands upon thousands of men, yet he who conquers himself is (truly) the greatest in battle.

It is indeed better to conquer oneself than to conquer other people.

Dhammapada 103–4

9

THE PRINCES AND THE BARBER

WHEN THE BUDDHA first arrived in the land of the Sakyans, they were very suspicious of him and either met him with a rather stiff formality or avoided him altogether. It did not take long, though, for people to be won over by his kindness and by the simple but profound words of wisdom that he spoke. Soon they were flocking to hear him teach and to enjoy the feeling of peace that came from just sitting in his presence. Many became his disciples. Not only from within Gotama's own former family, but from within nearly all the noble families of the Sakyans, young men gave up their privileged way of life to follow the Buddha as homeless wanderers. When the Buddha decided it was time to leave Kapilavatthu and move on, he left accompanied by many of these young noblemen, now wearing the simple robes of a monk, and carrying staff and begging-bowl. The city felt strangely empty when they had gone, and life would never be the same again for the Sakyan people.

Soon after the Buddha's departure, a Sakyan prince called Mahanama sat in his palace garden. He reflected that no one from his family had yet taken up the homeless life as a disciple of the Buddha, while from almost every other noble family at least one young man had become a monk. Mahanama had an urgent feeling that this was not right, and that something had to be done about it. He went off to find his younger brother Anuruddha and, finding him, took him by the arm and led him to a quiet corner of the garden, telling him there was something very important he needed to talk to him about. Mahanama told Anuruddha his thoughts. Mahanama had a wife and children, and would need to care for their widowed mother, but Anuruddha was still single and had few responsibilities. Mahanama proposed to Anuruddha that he think seriously about going off to join the Buddha.

Now Anuruddha was a refined youth who had so far enjoyed a very pleasant and sheltered life, and at first he did not like his brother's idea at all. Mahanama was persuasive and persistent, however, pointing out the endless responsibilities and work that burdened a householder's life, and Anuruddha was gradually won over. Indeed, he became convinced that it was only by renouncing his present life and following the Buddha that he would ever find real happiness.

So Anuruddha went to his mother to ask her permission to go forth and join the Buddha. At first she would not hear of it, and now it was Anuruddha's turn to be persuasive and persistent. Eventually his mother said, 'All right, my dear Anuruddha, all right. Have your own way, but on one condition. If your friend Bhaddiya goes forth, then you too shall go forth.' Bhaddiya, Anuruddha's best friend, was a prince, and one of the chosen leaders of the Sakyans. Anuruddha's mother saw no likelihood whatsoever of Bhaddiya giving even a second thought to taking up the spiritual life, and she was confident that that would be the end of the matter.

Anuruddha, however, had other ideas. He set off straight away to find his friend. As soon as they met Anuruddha seized Bhaddiya's hands and declared, 'My going forth depends on yours!' Bhaddiya was taken aback by the urgency of Anuruddha's speech and the force of feeling behind it. Without thinking, he responded immediately, 'I will not stop your going forth. You and I will ...' Then, realizing what he was saying, he stopped abruptly, and changed tack. 'Well, yes, you must go forth whenever you want.'

'Let us go forth together.'

'I can't go forth. You know that. The Sakyans have chosen me as one of their leaders. I will do anything else for you, my friend, but I cannot do that. You go forth.'

'My mother has said I can only go forth if you do. You said quite clearly that you would not stop my going forth, so let us go together to join the Buddha.'

The Sakyans were known to be men of their word, and Bhaddiya was no exception. He had said he would not prevent his friend going forth, and he now felt bound to honour his word. He found himself in a very awkward position and proposed a compromise.

'All right,' he said, 'Wait for seven years, and then we shall go forth together.'

'That is much too long.'

'Then six years.'

That was still far too long for Anuruddha to wait. Bhaddiya tried for five years, four years, three years, two years, one year, but each time Anuruddha protested that he could not wait that long.

'Then seven months ... two months ... two weeks.'

It was still too long for Anuruddha.

'Then seven days. Wait seven days for me to hand over my duties to my children and my brothers, and then we shall go forth together.'

Anuruddha agreed to wait seven days.

After seven days, Bhaddiya and Anuruddha, together with four other princes to whom they had secretly confided their plan to go forth, set out from Kapilavatthu leading a company of troops. The other four, who had decided to join them and go forth too, were called Ananda, Bhagu, Kimbila, and Devadatta. The sight of the princes taking the army out on exercise was very familiar to the Sakyans. It meant that life was going on as normal. When they had travelled a good way from the city, however, the princes called a halt. They gave orders to the soldiers to about-turn and march back to Kapilavatthu. Taking with them only their servant, the barber Upali, they journeyed until they came to the river that marked the edge of the Sakyan territory.

There the princes took off all their royal insignia and rolled them up in a cloak. They gave the cloak to Upali and charged him to take it back to Kapilavatthu and tell the Sakyans they had decided to go forth and join the Buddha. Then, bidding him farewell, they crossed over into the neighbouring kingdom. Upali was greatly surprised by this turn of events, but with customary obedience he shouldered the bundle and set off as the princes had bidden him in the direction of Kapilavatthu. As he walked along he reflected on this unexpected happening.

'The Sakyans are a fierce people,' he thought. 'When they find out what has happened they could easily put me to death for helping the princes go forth. I would be much better off joining them and going forth too.'

Thinking this, he hung the insignia on a tree and turned and hurried after them. He caught up with them, and they welcomed his decision with warm smiles.

Together they travelled on to find the Buddha. Everywhere he had been the people were full of talk of him, and his trail was not difficult to follow. Coming eventually into his presence, the six princes and the barber asked to enter his order of monks and be accepted as his disciples. When the Buddha agreed, the princes had a further request: they asked that Upali be ordained first. He had been their servant, but if he was ordained before them they would have to show him due respect and their fierce Sakyan pride would be humbled. The Buddha smiled. He understood very well the significance of their request, so he ordained Upali first, and the six princes after him.

Do not abandon yourselves to unmindfulness; have no intimacy with sensuous delights. The mindful person, absorbed in superconscious states, gains ample bliss.

As a dweller in the mountains looks down on those who live in the valley, so the spiritually mature person, the hero free from sorrow, having driven out unmindfulness by means of mindfulness, ascends to the Palace of Wisdom and looks down at the sorrowful, spiritually immature multitude (below).

Mindful among the unmindful, wide awake among the sleeping, the man of good understanding forges ahead like a swift horse outdistancing a feeble hack.

Dhammapada 27–9

10

ANATHAPINDIKA

IT WAS MORE THAN two-and-a-half years since the Buddha had gained Enlightenment. He already had many disciples, and his fame continued to spread. He was spending the time of the monsoon – when rain, mud, and floods made wandering difficult – in the Bamboo Grove near the city of Rajagaha. A rich merchant of the city was greatly impressed by the calm and mindful demeanour of the Buddha's followers and felt moved to help them. He asked the Buddha's permission to build shelters for them so they did not have to live out in the open, exposed to the elements. The Buddha agreed, the huts were built, and the Buddha and his monks were invited to a ceremonial meal during which the huts would be formally presented to them.

This merchant's wife had a brother known as Anathapindika, 'feeder of the poor', a wealthy and generous banker of the city of Savatthi. He arrived in Rajagaha on business the day before the ceremony was to take place. He found his brother-in-law busy giving orders to his servants and having them run to and fro, engrossed in preparations for the feast. Such were the scale and lavishness of the preparations that Anathapindika assumed there was to be a marriage, or some great religious offering, or a visit from the king and his retinue. Normally the merchant would have dropped everything to make his brother-in-law welcome, but today he seemed completely preoccupied with his task. Eventually all the orders were given and all the arrangements made. The merchant came over and greeted Anathapindika, who was very curious to know what was afoot.

'Oh no, there is no marriage or royal visit,' explained the merchant, 'but tomorrow the Buddha and his followers will be my guests.'

Anathapindika was awe-struck. 'Did you say the Buddha?' he asked again and again. 'Did you say the Buddha?'

The very word seemed to resonate through his entire being. He became very excited, and wanted to see the Buddha straightaway, but his brother-in-law persuaded him that now was not the appropriate time, as it was already getting late. The merchant promised Anathapindika that he would definitely see the Buddha first thing the following morning. Anathapindika reluctantly accepted that he would have to wait. He went to his room and got into bed, but his mind was racing.

'Early tomorrow I shall see the Buddha, an Enlightened One,' Anathapindika kept telling himself. He lay down but couldn't sleep, and he got up three times thinking it was already dawn. On the third occasion he got out of bed, dressed, and set off to see the Buddha, having convinced himself it was nearly light, although it was still the middle of the night.

The city gate was barred and the guard was asleep, but this did not stop Anathapindika. The gate was mysteriously opened for him by the magic powers of a yaksha who wanted to help him pursue his quest. Anathapindika set out towards the Bamboo Grove, where the Buddha was staying, but once he had left the security of the city the dark seemed to close in on him, and fear and terror overcame him. One moment he was frozen to the spot in terror, the next ready to run back to the city. Fortunately, the yaksha had accompanied Anathapindika and urged him on, an invisible voice of calm and resolve in his ear. Anathapindika hesitated. Then, taking courage, he overcame the feelings of panic and dread and continued on his way.

The Buddha was already up, walking in the Bamboo Grove. When he saw Anathapindika coming he greeted him by name, and invited him to sit with him. Anathapindika prostrated himself before the Buddha and took a seat beside him. Sitting together with the Buddha through the early hours of the morning, experiencing the immensity of his presence, hearing his words, sensing his boundless kindness and compassion, a new vision of existence and a new universe of understanding opened up for Anathapindika. He went for refuge to the Buddha and took him as his teacher.

The following day, Anathapindika had a meal prepared for the Buddha and his monks, and invited them to stay in

Savatthi for the remainder of the rainy season. He declared that he would personally see to it that all their needs were well taken care of.

When Anathapindika's business in Rajagaha was completed, he returned to Savatthi, and all along the way he told people about the Buddha and urged them to make him welcome when he travelled along that road. When he arrived back in Savatthi he looked for a suitable place for the Buddha and his disciples to stay. Eventually, he found a beautiful park, ideal in every way, owned by a prince by the name of Jeta. He went to the prince and asked him to sell him the park. 'The park will not be sold unless it is covered with 100,000 pieces of gold,' declared Prince Jeta, not thinking for one moment that anyone would take such an outrageous demand seriously. 'The park is taken,' was Anathapindika's immediate response. 'Oh no it's not!' snapped back Prince Jeta, taken aback at this turn of events. Anathapindika, however, pressed his case, and it was taken to arbitration. A price had been stated and met, the man's word was his bond, so the elders of Savatthi declared that the park was Anathapindika's if he could indeed cover it with gold coins. Cart-loads of gold were spread over the park, until only a small space near the gate was left. Anathapindika was about to send carts for more gold when Prince Jeta, by now realizing this was no ordinary matter, called to him, 'Enough, householder. Enough. Leave that space. Let it be my gift.' Happy to encourage others in devotion to the Buddha, Anathapindika accepted the gift, and Prince Jeta built a gate there.

The Buddha came to Savatthi, and over the years that followed he spent many rainy seasons in the Jeta Grove. Anathapindika continued to be a faithful and generous friend and disciple to the Buddha throughout his life. At one point reduced to poverty through bad luck in business and by his unstinting generosity, Anathapindika's only regret was that he did not have more to give. He is remembered as one of the greatest of the Buddha's lay followers.

Be quick to do what is (morally) beautiful.
Restrain the mind from evil. He who is sluggish
in doing good, his mind delights in evil.

Should a man (once) do evil, let him not make
a habit of it; let him not set his heart on it.
Painful is the heaping up of evil.

Should a man (once) do good, let him make
a habit of it; let him set his heart on it.
Happy is the heaping up of good.

Dhammapada 116–8

11

QUARRELLING MONKS

EVEN IN THE EARLY DAYS of the Buddhist community, the presence of the Buddha was not always enough to prevent his disciples falling out and becoming prey to anger and ignorance. The first split to seriously threaten the community took place around ten years after the Buddha's Enlightenment, and began with a petty incident among the monks living at a place called Kosambi.

There were two monks of long standing in this community, one of them an expert in the rules of the life of the community, the other an expert in the teachings. One day the expert in teachings went to the latrine and left a vessel there containing some unused water. The expert in rules went along just after him and, finding the water there, asked the expert in teachings if it was he who had left it. He admitted it was.

'You realize, don't you, that it is against the rules of this community to leave water in the latrine?'

'I didn't know that, but if I have broken a rule, I will

confess it.'

'Well, if it was done unintentionally or out of forgetfulness, it wasn't an offence.'

They parted, with the expert on the teachings thinking that since he had not technically broken the rules of the community that was the end of the matter.

However, the expert in rules later told his pupils that the expert on teachings did not know when he had committed an offence. They in turn told the pupils of the other monk, 'Do you realize that your preceptor has committed an offence and thinks he hasn't?'

The pupils of the expert on teachings related this to their teacher, who responded angrily, 'The expert on rules said to me that I had not committed an offence, and now he is telling others that I did. He is a liar!'

This outburst was soon reported back to the pupils of the expert on rules. 'Your preceptor is a liar!'

When this reached the ears of the expert on rules he was outraged, and immediately called a chapter meeting and had the expert on teachings suspended from the order. The expert on the teachings, however, was a monk of long standing, with considerable influence and many friends. He quickly rallied support to his side and soon the community for miles around was being drawn into the dispute by one side or the other. The divisions quickly became deeper and more entrenched, the feelings more bitter, and things went from bad to worse.

When word of this quarrel reached the Buddha he was deeply concerned and went straight to Kosambi to meet the monks. He summoned the quarrelling monks from both sides and tried to reason with them, but to no avail. They even asked the Buddha to leave them to sort the matter out and not to interfere. Faced with such stubbornness and stupidity he saw there was nothing more to be done and, greatly saddened, he returned alone to Savatthi.

The conflict raged on, and eventually the lay followers in Kosambi, hearing that the quarrelling monks had ignored even the Buddha, withdrew their support. When the Kosambi monks went on their almsround they found themselves shunned at every door. With their begging-bowls and their stomachs empty, they finally came to their senses. They agreed to go to Savatthi and settle their dispute in the presence of the Buddha.

News of the arrival of the quarrelling monks at Savatthi was greeted with great apprehension by the disciples there. They would rather have had nothing to do with them, but the Buddha gave explicit instructions that the Kosambi monks should be received, lodged, fed, and treated with utmost respect and fairness. Meetings were arranged, and the Buddha, with great patience, calm, and objectivity, discussed the issues with the monks.

Gradually the heat of anger subsided, and the monks on both sides were able to see more clearly what had happened and how the quarrel had developed. The expert on teachings was able to put aside his pride and acknowledge his fault in the affair, accept his suspension, and ask the Buddha to reinstate him. The expert in rules was also able to confess his unskilfulness and a friendly settlement was made. The two sides were reconciled and the community of monks was once more at peace.

Those who entertain such thoughts as 'He abused me, he beat me, he conquered me, he robbed me,' will not still their hatred.

Those who do not entertain such thoughts as 'He abused me, he beat me, he conquered me, he robbed me,' will still their hatred.

Not by hatred are hatreds ever pacified here (in the world). They are pacified by love. This is the eternal law.

Others do not realize that we are all heading for death. Those who do realize it will compose their quarrels.

Dhammapada 3–6

12

PERFECT BROTHERHOOD

WHEN THE BUDDHA failed in his first attempt to resolve the dispute between the monks at Kosambi, he left them and went alone into the forest for a while. On his way back towards Savatthi he visited the Eastern Bamboo Park, where three of his followers, Anuruddha, Nandiya, and Kimbila were living and practising. This was the same Anuruddha who had persuaded Bhaddiya to go forth with him, and who, together with Kimbila and the other princes, had secretly left Kapilavatthu to become disciples of the Buddha. The beauty and simplicity of the life the three friends enjoyed together stood in strong contrast to the quarrelling and wrangling of the Kosambi bhikkhus.

As the Buddha approached the park he was stopped by the park-keeper who, not knowing who he was, asked him not to disturb the three monks living there and striving for liberation. Anuruddha heard the park-keeper conversing with the Buddha and came out to reassure him. 'Thank you friend, but don't worry. This is the Buddha, our teacher, who has come to visit us.' Anuruddha then summoned his friends, telling them the Buddha had come to visit them. With great happiness in their hearts they welcomed him, paid their respects, prepared a seat, took his outer robe and bowl, and brought water for him to wash his feet. They sat together, and the Buddha asked if they were all well and comfortable, and having no trouble in collecting food. Anuruddha assured him that all was well.

'I hope you all live together in harmony, Anuruddha, as friendly and free of differences as milk and water blended together, looking on each other with kindly eyes.'

'Indeed we do, Lord.'

'And how do you live in this way Anuruddha?'

Anuruddha replied, 'I consider myself very fortunate to have such companions in the holy life. In each and every act of body, speech, and mind I extend loving kindness towards them. I think, 'Why not put aside what I want to do and do only what they want to do.' We may be separate in body, Lord, but truly we are of one mind.'

The other two each said exactly the same as Anuruddha.

'Good, good, Anuruddha. And I hope you are living mindful and self-controlled, practising earnestly and with bright energy.'

'Indeed we are Lord.'

'And how do you live in this way?'

'Well, Lord, whichever of us gets back first from their almsround in the village gets the seat ready, sets out water for drinking and for washing, and puts the refuse bucket ready. Whoever returns last eats as much of the remaining food as he wants, and throws the rest away where nothing grows or into water where there is no life. He puts away the seats and the water, puts away the refuse bucket, and sweeps the eating area. Whenever one of us notices that the pots of water for drinking or washing or for the latrine are empty, he refills them. If they are too heavy for him he signals with his hand for help. We don't speak over such matters. But every fifth night we sit together discussing the teachings. In this way we live mindful and self-controlled, practising earnestly and with bright energy.'

The Buddha was pleased by what he heard. He now went on to ask the three friends how they were progressing on the path towards wisdom. They told him how, although in many ways their meditation practice was going very well, there seemed to be a point beyond which they just could not progress. Having become concentrated they would encounter an inner light, which again and again slipped away from them. The Buddha urged them to look more closely at their own minds and learn to recognize the various hindrances that can arise in meditation. He described in great detail the obstacles such as doubt and distraction, fear and elation, that he himself had had to learn to overcome before being able to pass beyond them to attain knowledge and vision of things as they really are.

When the Buddha had answered all their questions, and given them all the guidance he could, warm farewells were exchanged, and he went on his way to Savatthi, leaving the three friends to their spiritual striving in the Eastern Bamboo Park.

Happy indeed we live, friendly amid the haters. Among men who hate we dwell free from hate.

Happy indeed we live, healthy amid the sick. Among men who are sick we dwell free from sickness.

Happy indeed we live, content amid the greedy. Among men who are greedy we dwell free from greed.

Dhammapada 197–9

13

THE PLOUGHMAN

THE BUDDHA was once staying in the kingdom of Magadha, near a village called Ekanala. It was sowing time, and a wealthy brahmin called Kasi Bharadvaja had 500 teams of oxen and ploughs and many labourers at work on his land. The Buddha went to beg for food while the landowner was feeding his workers. Seeing the Buddha standing with his bowl, Bharadvaja called to him. 'Holy man, I plough and I sow, and having ploughed and sown, I eat. If you will do some ploughing and sowing, holy man, you can eat too!' He was prepared to feed a wandering holy man, but only if he did a day's work like everyone else.

The Buddha replied, 'I plough too, brahmin, and I sow, and when I have ploughed and sown, I eat.' The brahmin was a hearty character and he enjoyed this exchange. 'I do not see your oxen or yoke or plough or goad, Master Gotama, yet you say that you plough and sow and eat. You will have to tell us what sort of farmer you are!'

The Buddha now gave voice to inspired words that rang out like a song:

Faith is the seed I sow, and self-control is my rein.
Wisdom is my yoke and plough.
Conscience is my guiding pole, and mind is the rope I hold.
Mindfulness is my goad.
Guarded in every act of body and of speech,
Moderate in what I eat,
With truth I destroy all weeds.
In calm I find release.
Energy is the yoked oxen
That carries me to perfect freedom
Without my ever looking back.
This is the ploughing that I do,
And it has the Deathless as its fruit.
Whoever ploughs like this will be freed from all suffering.

Kasi Bharadvaja was impressed and pleased with this reply, and he ordered a fine bronze bowl to be filled with milk rice and brought to the Buddha. The Buddha, however, refused it. A Buddha does not sing for his supper, he explained, and he would not accept any payment for his declaration of the Truth.

'So to whom shall I give this bowl of food?' asked the brahmin, becoming exasperated at the holy man's seeming contrariness. The Buddha replied that he saw no one in the whole world apart from an Enlightened One or one of his disciples who would be able to digest the food; Bharadvaja had better throw it away on some barren land or into water where there was no life. The brahmin rather scornfully threw the milk rice into a ditch of stagnant water. As soon as the rice entered the water it started to steam and hiss and boil violently, as if a white-hot ploughshare that had been heated in a forge for a whole day had been dropped into it. The brahmin was terrified. He ran to the Buddha, prostrated before him, and asked him to accept him as a disciple. There and then, leaving behind all his land and wealth, Kạsi Bharadvaja became a homeless wanderer.

Later, living alone in the forest and practising with great effort and determination, he gained Enlightenment.

That infatuated man whose delight is in offspring and cattle, death goes and carries him off as a great flood (sweeps away) a sleeping village.

Sons are no protection, nor father, nor yet (other) relatives. For him who is seized by the End-maker (i.e., Death), there is no protection forthcoming from relatives.

Knowing the significance of this, let the spiritually mature person, the man restrained by good conduct, speedily cleanse the Way leading to Nirvana.

Dhammapada 287–9

14

THE BEAUTIFUL MANGO GROVE

THE BUDDHA SPENT the thirteenth rainy season after his Enlightenment at Chalika, and with him, as his attendant, was a young monk called Meghiya. One day Meghiya went to a nearby village to beg for food. As he was slowly returning along the banks of the River Kimikala, he came across a beautiful shady mango grove, with a delicate fragrance hanging in the air, a peaceful and truly delightful spot. 'This,' thought Meghiya, 'is the perfect place to meditate. It is the perfect place to gain Enlightenment.' He imagined himself sitting under a tree, enjoying blissful meditation.

Returning to the Buddha in a mood of urgency and excitement, Meghiya told him about the beautiful mango grove he had discovered, and asked his permission to go there and strive for Enlightenment.

'Wait Meghiya,' the Buddha replied, 'I am alone here. Wait until another monk comes.' But Meghiya had set his heart on going to the mango grove, and was too impatient to heed the Buddha's request. He asked the Buddha again, and a second time the Buddha asked him to wait. Unswayed, Meghiya put his request a third time, saying, 'Lord, you have already done all there is to be done. For you the victory is won.' But I still have the goal of the spiritual life to strive for.' At this, the Buddha, seeing his young disciple was not to be dissuaded, replied, 'All right Meghiya. If you really want to strive you had better go.'

Meghiya went off to the beautiful mango grove and seated himself at the foot of a tree to meditate. He was sure that Enlightenment could not be far away, and expected to find himself effortlessly rising into lofty states of consciousness. These states proved elusive, however, and Meghiya found himself caught up in thoughts of lust, hatred, and cruelty. He struggled again and again to free himself from them, but to no avail. Sobered by his failure, he sat and reflected on the irony that this should happen after he had given up everything to pursue the spiritual path. He had committed himself to a simple life, found this beautiful spot, and sat himself down to meditate, only to find his mind filled with thoughts such as these!

Humbled, he returned that same evening to the Buddha and told him all that had happened. The Buddha was kind but firm in his response to the young monk. 'When the heart's release is immature, Meghiya,' he explained, 'there are five things that bring about maturity. The first is a spiritual friend; a good companion in the holy life. The second is training in perfect morality and conduct. The third is engagement in appropriate talk. Such talk is unselfish, and concerns the heart's release, freedom, and

Enlightenment. It is talk on wanting little, on contentment, seclusion, energy, morality, meditation, wisdom, liberation, and knowledge and vision of things as they really are. The fourth thing that conduces to maturity of the heart's release is energy and effort in abandoning states of mind that are lustful, angry, and confused, and the development of clear mental states full of generosity and love. One needs to develop stamina and persistence in cultivating such positive mental states. The fifth thing is the development of understanding and insight that will lead eventually to the wisdom and insight of the Buddhas. A monk who has a spiritual friend, who has a good companion in the holy life, will cultivate morality and helpful talk, and will develop energy and gain insight.'

As Meghiya listened to the Buddha he felt humbled, and embarrassed at his own arrogance and naivety. He realized that Enlightenment would not simply fall into his lap – as if out of the trees – while he sat meditating in a beautiful mango grove, but that he had a lot of hard work to do. He also felt immense gratitude as he realized that in the Buddha he already had the first of the five necessary things, a spiritual friend and teacher who was both wise and kind.

Good it is to see the spiritually developed; to (actually) dwell with them is always happiness. By not seeing the spiritually immature, one indeed will be perpetually happy.

By living in company with the spiritually immature one grieves for a long time. Association with the spiritually immature is always painful, like association with an enemy. Association with the wise is pleasant, like the coming together of relatives.

(Therefore it is said:) Follow after him who is wise, understanding, and learned, who bears the yoke of virtue, is religious and spiritually developed. Follow after one of such a nature, as the moon follows the path of the stars.

Dhammapada 206–8

15

ANGULIMALA

TWENTY YEARS had passed since the Buddha's Enlightenment. Each year he spent the rainy season in the Jeta Grove at Savatthi. One year, a cruel and murderous robber appeared in the kingdom of Kosala. He indiscriminately attacked, robbed, and killed whoever crossed his path, cutting a finger off each of his victims. These fingers he strung together and wore in a gruesome necklace, so he was known as Angulimala or 'finger-necklace'. Wherever he went, people fled in terror, and whole towns and villages were left deserted.

One morning, having begged his meal in Savatthi, the Buddha set out down the road towards the district Angulimala was known to be terrorizing. As he walked, the Buddha was warned by farmers, cowherds, goat-herds, and travellers not to go that way. Bands of ten, twenty, thirty, even forty had tried to get through, hoping to find safety in numbers, but all had fallen into the cruel and dreadful hands of Angulimala and perished. The Buddha heard their warnings, but paid no heed and walked on in silence.

Angulimala had found a vantage point from which he could keep watch over the road to Savatthi, but for hours he had seen only a stray dog and a few wild animals. The road was completely empty. Then in the distance he made out a solitary figure walking slowly in his direction. As the figure drew closer Angulimala saw that he was wearing a monk's robe. He could not believe that a monk would be so foolish as to travel alone down a road where he was known to have vanquished bands of as many as forty travellers. Had nobody warned him? Or did he expect his gods to protect him? Angulimala did not care. Whether he was a brave man or a fool, he would have this monk's life. Grabbing his sword and shield and bow and arrows he climbed down and set off towards him.

As Angulimala came closer to the monk, he broke out of the forest on to the road and sprinted after him, intending to run him down. But something remarkable happened. No matter how quickly he ran, he was unable to catch up with the Buddha, who continued to walk calmly and steadily down the road. Angulimala was perplexed. 'Usually I can catch a galloping elephant or horse, a chariot or a deer, yet this monk continues to walk along at his ordinary pace, and I can't catch him!' He tried to run faster, but still the gap between him and his quarry did not decrease.

Eventually he stopped and shouted out after the Buddha, 'Stop, monk, stop!' The Buddha replied, 'I have stopped Angulimala. Now you must stop too!' and he continued walking. This perplexed Angulimala even more. He guessed from his appearance that this man was a follower of the Buddha, and his disciples were supposed never to lie. Yet this monk said he had stopped when he was still walking, and he was telling Angulimala that he must stop when he was already standing still. He demanded that the monk explain himself.

'Angulimala, I have stopped all violence towards living beings, but you know no restraint at all. That is why I have stopped and you have not.' Hearing these words, Angulimala was shaken. He knew that here at last, in this fearless monk, was a teacher he could respect. The time had come for him to renounce his evil ways. He threw away his weapons and fell at the Buddha's feet, begging him to accept him as a disciple. With head shaved and wearing the ragged robe of a forest monk, Angulimala returned with the Buddha to Savatthi.

Meanwhile, in the city, a restive crowd was clamouring at the palace gates for King Pasenadi to do something about the murderous robber who was terrorizing the countryside. So the king rode out with a band of 500 men, and on nearing the Jeta Grove he dismounted and walked over to see the Buddha, of whom he had long been a disciple.

'What troubles you, good king,' the Buddha asked, 'Is your kingdom invaded?' Pasenadi told him of the terrible robber and murderer who was laying waste the countryside, and whom he despaired of ever capturing. 'What if Angulimala were to abandon his life of killing and crime, shave his head and put on the monk's robe and become my disciple. What would you do then?' asked the Buddha. 'I would show him the respect due a monk, and see that his needs were met. But, Lord, Angulimala is too set on his evil ways ever to change.'

Extending his arm in the direction of a monk sitting close by, the Buddha said, 'Good king, this is Angulimala.' Pasenadi was shocked and terrified; his hair stood on end and he shook with fear. The Buddha reassured him. 'Do not be afraid, good king, do not be afraid. There is nothing to fear.' The king's horror gradually subsided and he regained his composure. He went over to Angulimala, paid formal respects to him, and asked him if there was anything he needed.

Returning to the Buddha, he expressed his wonder and gratitude that the Buddha had managed by peaceful means to tame Angulimala when all the power and force at his own disposal had failed. King Pasenadi returned to his palace a much happier man, and his people went back to their homes and felt safe again.

Angulimala now followed the life of a monk, and went every morning to beg his food in Savatthi. During one almsround he came to a house where a young woman was enduring a very painful and difficult labour. Compassion was aroused in him, and he felt keenly for the suffering of the woman and her child. When he returned he spoke of this with the Buddha. 'Go back to the city,' the Buddha told him, 'and say to the woman, "Sister, since I was born I have not intentionally taken the life of any living being. By that truth may you and the child find peace."'

'Lord, that would be a lie, for I have deliberately taken the life of many beings.'

'Then, Angulimala, go to Savatthi and say to the woman, "Since I was born in the noble birth I have not intentionally taken the life of any living being. By that truth may you and the child find peace."'

Angulimala did this, and the woman and her child found peace.

The Buddha carefully watched over his new disciple's progress in the spiritual life, and when he considered him ready he sent Angulimala into the forest to meditate alone. Practising with great determination and energy he soon gained full Enlightenment.

One day while begging in Savatthi, Angulimala was recognized by people who had reason to hate him for his past deeds. They angrily threw sticks, stones, clods of earth, and broken pots at him, calling him a murderer. He returned to the Buddha with his head gashed and bleeding, his bowl broken, his robe torn. The Buddha saw him coming and went to meet him saying, 'Bear it noble one, bear it. You are experiencing here and now the ripening of karma for which you might otherwise have suffered in hellish existences for thousands of years in future lives.'

Alone in retreat, enjoying the bliss of liberation, Angulimala uttered a prayer that his enemies, too, might find the teaching of the Buddha, and know the peace and happiness that he now knew.

Do not underestimate evil, (thinking) 'It will not approach me.' A water-pot becomes full by the (constant) falling of drops of water. (Similarly) the spiritually immature person little by little fills himself with evil.

Do not underestimate good, (thinking) 'It will not approach me.' A water-pot becomes full by the (constant) falling of drops of water. (Similarly) the wise man little by little fills himself with good.

As a merchant (travelling) with a small caravan and much wealth avoids a dangerous road, or as one desirous of life shuns poison, so should one keep clear of evil.

If one has no wound in one's hand one may (safely) handle poison. The unwounded hand is not affected by poison. (Similarly) no evil befalls him who does no wrong.

Dhammapada 121–4

16

A YOUTHFUL CHALLENGE

THE BUDDHA was touring the kingdom of Kosala accompanied by a large number of monks, when they came to a brahmin village called Opasada. As was their custom, they stayed just outside the village, in a pleasant grove of sal trees. Opasada was a prosperous village, ruled by a brahmin called Chanki, whom King Pasenadi had granted the power to govern in his name. As word got around that the Buddha had arrived in the village and was staying in the sal grove, brahmin householders poured out of the village and along the road to see him. A visit from a well-known holy man was something not to be missed.

Chanki was taking a rest on the roof of his palace in the afternoon heat. He saw the crowd streaming out of the village and wanted to know what was going on. His servant told him that Gotama the Buddha was in the sal grove, whereupon Chanki decided that he too would visit the famous sage. He sent the servant to tell the other householders to wait so that he could go along with them.

At that time, a number of important brahmins from neighbouring districts were visiting Opasada on business, and when they heard of Chanki's intention to visit the Buddha they were not at all happy. They went to his palace to try to dissuade him. 'Please do not visit the wanderer Gotama,' they begged, 'It is not appropriate that the noble Chanki should visit Gotama. Rather it is Gotama who should be coming to pay his respects to Chanki.' They were concerned that a brahmin of the rank and distinction of Chanki should not be seen putting himself in a subservient position to a wandering holy man like Gotama.

There were two distinct religious traditions in ancient India at the time of the Buddha. One was the tradition of the Vedas, whose lore and ritual was handed down from generation to generation by the priestly brahmin caste, who jealously guarded it as their preserve. The other was the colourful and diverse tradition of the shramanas, the wandering holy men, who were concerned not with the venerable Vedic tradition, but with direct spiritual experience, which they sought in a myriad different ways. The two traditions existed side by side, and to some extent overlapped, but at times there was inevitably some rivalry. The concern of the visiting brahmins was that by visiting the shramana Gotama, Chanki may appear to be acknowledging that a shramana could be wiser and holier than a brahmin.

Chanki, however, was not troubled by such concerns and resisted their opposition. He insisted that he would go and see the Buddha, and furthermore that the brahmins who had come to petition him should accompany him. As a man in Chanki's position was not to be argued with, they had no choice but to follow.

Thus, with a large company of brahmins, Chanki went to the sal grove. Respectful greetings were exchanged, people seated themselves, and the Buddha entered into discussion on various matters with a number of learned and well-respected brahmins. Among the brahmins who had accompanied Chanki was an exceptional youth called Kapathika. Though only sixteen, he had already completed his brahminical training and was recognized as a master in the Vedas. He joined in the conversation, which led the Buddha to rebuke him for speaking out of turn, before his elders. At this, Chanki spoke up for the youth, pointing out that he was already a recognized master of the Vedas and therefore, despite his age, it was quite appropriate that he should join the discussion. The Buddha, realizing that he must indeed be an exceptional young man, allowed him to continue to participate.

Kapathika, growing in confidence and keen to make his mark, now caught the Buddha's attention and asked him a question: 'Master Gotama, according to the tradition of the brahmins, all truth is to be found in the Vedas and nowhere else. What do you have to say to that?' The traditions of the brahmins and the shramanas were now in direct, if polite, confrontation. The Buddha responded immediately and directly. 'Is there anyone among all you brahmins who can say, "I know this. I have seen this truth for myself and know it with certainty to be so"? Is there any among your teachers who can say this, or among their teachers going back over the generations, or even among the ancient sages? Do not even the ancient sages always refer back to their teacher before them? Are you brahmins, then, not like a string of blind men holding each others' shirt-tails, with neither those at the front nor those at the back able to see anything for themselves? Your faith in your tradition would seem to have little basis.'

At this, those brahmins who had tried to persuade Chanki not to visit the Buddha caught their breath. Their worst fears were being realized and the shramana was making them look like fools. 'If only that boy had kept his mouth shut!' they muttered to one another. But it was too late for that, and Kapathika was not going to admit defeat so easily. 'Good Gotama, we brahmins do not rely just on our faith in the tradition. We also listen carefully to what it has to say.'

For his part, the Buddha did not intend to let Kapathika off the hook. 'First you mention faith in the tradition, and now you speak of listening to what the tradition has to say. We can speak of five things: faith, inclination, listening to what is said, rational consideration, and reflection on and liking an opinion, and we can say they are all grounds for holding something to be true. But look more carefully. One can have faith that something is true, and it can still be untrue. Or one can have faith that something is untrue, and it can be true. It is the same with each of these grounds; with inclination, listening to what is said, rational consideration, and reflection on and liking an opinion. Each may be a basis for provisionally holding something to be true, but we must be clear that that is not the same as awakening to the truth. It is not the same as really knowing something to be true in the depths of your own being.'

'And how then, good Gotama, does this awakening to the truth that you speak of come about?' asked Kapathika. In response, the Buddha clearly set out for the youth the whole process of the spiritual life. He said to him, 'Suppose a wandering holy man comes to your village or town. First of all you must look closely at him. You must ask yourself if his behaviour is consistent with what you would expect of one who is free from greed, hatred, and delusion. You must look at what he teaches, and ask yourself if this is really the teaching of one who is free from greed, hatred, and delusion. You must ask if following these teachings is really going to lead people to freedom or into greater ensnarement. When you are satisfied on all these counts, then faith in that holy man begins to flower, and you can draw closer and listen carefully to his teachings.

'Remember the teachings, test their meaning in the light of reason, and make sure you understand them. This will give rise in turn to a desire to realize them more fully and deeply. Motivated by this desire, you will make a real effort to put them into practice. Then, after a while, you will need to stop and assess your progress. Are you still convinced that the teacher is free from greed, hatred, and delusion, and that these teachings are indeed leading you towards freedom? If, having weighed things up, your faith in your teacher and the path is confirmed, then listen further. Take on more teachings, and energetically apply yourself to their practice. In time, stop once more and assess your progress. Continuing in this way you will eventually reach a point where your faith in the teaching and the path is firm. Then, giving yourself wholeheartedly to your practice and striving resolutely, you will awaken to the truth.'

The brahmin youth was pleased with the Buddha's answers but he wanted to know more. The Buddha had so far spoken only of awakening to truth. What of the attainment of truth? What of full realization?

'Just more of the same. The whole process of the spiritual life as I have described it must be lived out ever more deeply, ever more fully and completely.'

Kapathika was satisfied, and at the same time his youthful pride was humbled. He realized the narrowness of the brahmin tradition to which he had thus far adhered, and a new respect for the path of the shramana awoke within him. Recognizing in the Buddha a teacher whose wisdom far outshone anything he had previously encountered, he there and then asked to be accepted as a lay disciple.

Better than a thousand meaningless words collected together (in the Vedic oral tradition) is a single meaningful word on hearing which one becomes tranquil.

Better than a thousand meaningless verses collected together (in the Vedic oral tradition) is one (meaningful) line of verse on hearing which one becomes tranquil.

Dhammapada 100–1

17

LITTLE UGLY

THE BUDDHA was an immensely skilful teacher. He could engage in sophisticated debate with philosophers and brahmins, and he could use down-to-earth analogies when speaking to farmers and countryfolk. Sometimes he would tell amusing tales involving the gods and goblins that peopled the universe of ancient India. Thus, while staying at the Jeta Grove, the Buddha once told this story to some of his disciples.

A long time ago, in the realm of the gods, an extremely ugly, pot-bellied dwarf yaksha appeared seated on the throne of Sakka, the king of the gods. Seeing this, the gods became annoyed. They got very worked up and indignant at this outrageous intrusion and began to insult the yaksha, telling him what they thought of his audacity. To their astonishment, however, the more angry and annoyed they got with the yaksha, the less ugly he became. Eventually, a very beautiful and handsome creature was seated on Sakka's throne.

Confused and bewildered by this, the gods went and found Sakka and related what had happened. 'Aha!' said Sakka, 'He must be a yaksha who feeds on anger!' He led the gods back to his palace and stood before the throne looking at the beautiful creature sitting there. He knelt respectfully before the yaksha and introduced himself as Sakka, king of the gods. He continued to talk, and the more polite and respectful he was, the more ugly the yaksha became, the more pot-bellied and dwarfish, until finally he vanished completely.

Sakka then declared to all the gods who had gathered to witness the spectacle that it was a long time since he had given way to anger. Harsh and angry words had no place in his life because he had trained himself always to hold his anger in check, and in this way he carefully guarded and assured his spiritual progress.

I call him a charioteer who holds back the arisen anger as though (holding back) a swerving chariot. Others are only holders of reins.

Overcome the angry by non-anger; overcome the wicked with good. Overcome the miserly by giving, the teller of lies with truth.

Dhammapada 222–3

18

PRIDESTIFF

AT ONE TIME there lived in Savatthi a brahmin who was known to everyone as Pridestiff (Manathaddha in Pali), because he was always so full of himself and of his own importance that he looked down on everyone else. He even refused to show the respect traditionally due to mother, father, teacher, and older brother, and instead expected everyone to defer to him.

One day, the Buddha was teaching in Savatthi, surrounded by a large crowd. Pridestiff was out walking and came upon the Buddha. Surveying the scene, he thought, 'There is the famous wanderer Gotama teaching in the middle of that crowd. I will go and sit near him. If he speaks to me I will be happy to speak to him, but if he doesn't speak to me I certainly won't be the first to speak!'

Pridestiff made his way through the crowd and sat down near the Buddha, but the Buddha took no notice of him and carried on with his teaching. Pridestiff waited as he had resolved, but after a while he got tired of being ignored.

'This wanderer Gotama doesn't know anything about anything, ignoring someone like me!' he thought, and decided to leave.

The Buddha, however, was well aware what was going on in Pridestiff's mind, and just as the brahmin made to go, he turned and looked him the eye. He spoke directly to Pridestiff, with a voice firm but kind. 'It is not good to foster pride, friend. If there is someone here whom you came to see, you had better pay him your respects.'

Pridestiff realized that the Buddha had read his thoughts, and the shock of just those few words shattered his fragile vanity. He fell on his face at the Buddha's feet, kissing and stroking them and saying his name. 'I am Pridestiff, Master Gotama, I am Pridestiff.'

The crowd was astonished. People could not believe what was taking place before their very eyes. 'Isn't that Pridestiff, who will never show respect where it is due, not to mother, father, teacher, or elder brother? Yet look at him now. Just look at the way he prostrates and humbles himself in front of Master Gotama.'

The Buddha said to Pridestiff, 'That is enough, brahmin. That is enough. Get up off the ground and take your seat here next to me.' Pridestiff did as he was told and sat down, a humbled and changed man. A few moments later, when he had had time to collect himself and reflect a little on what he had just experienced, Pridestiff spoke to the Buddha. As he spoke, he confessed the foolishness of his behaviour in the past, and declared that he could now see clearly the importance of showing respect to one's parents, teacher, and elder brother, and above all, he proclaimed, he could see the importance of respecting and venerating the Enlightened Ones.

He then asked the Buddha to accept him as a lay disciple from that day on – and for the rest of his life.

He who reverences those worthy of reverence, whether Enlightened Ones or (their) disciples, (men) who have transcended illusion, and passed beyond grief and lamentation,

he who reverences those who are of such a nature, who (moreover) are at peace and without cause for fear, his merit is not to be reckoned as such and such.

Dhammapada 195–6

19

SONA'S SORE FEET

IN THE KINGDOM of Magadha, which was ruled over by King Bimbisara, lived Sona, the son of a nobleman. This young man was so refined and delicate that hair grew on the soles of his feet.

One day, King Bimbisara called an assembly of representatives from each of the villages in his kingdom and summoned Sona. He was curious to see this youth with hair on the soles of his feet whose fame had reached even as far as the palace. When the royal summons arrived, Sona's parents felt great pride but also some anxiety. They gave their son very careful instructions as to how he should behave in the royal presence. On no account was he to stretch his feet out towards the king, as that would be disrespectful. Rather he should sit cross-legged with the soles of his feet pointing up, so that the king could clearly see them. Accordingly, Sona went to the assembly and carefully did as his parents had instructed him. In this way

Bimbisara was able to see the famous youth with hair on the soles of his feet, and his royal curiosity was satisfied.

When the meeting with the village representatives was over, the king sent them to see the Buddha saying, 'I have told you how to manage the affairs of this mundane life. Now you must go to the Buddha and let him instruct you in the spiritual life.' Sona accompanied the village representatives to the Vulture's Peak, not far from the royal city of Rajagaha. Here he met the Buddha, and his life was transformed. He was so moved by the Buddha's teachings that he remained behind after all the villagers had left, and asked the Buddha to admit him to the order of monks.

Not long afterwards, he went to live alone in a nearby spot called the Cool Grove. Here he strove to make progress in his spiritual life. As he paced up and down, grappling with the Buddha's teachings and trying to understand how to apply them, his delicate feet became blistered and began to bleed. Soon there was a trail of blood where he had been walking, but Sona continued regardless, striving ever harder for understanding.

Some of the monks saw this, and were disturbed that one of their brethren should injure himself through his efforts. They reported this back to the Buddha, who went to see Sona.

'When you were alone in retreat just now, Sona, did you find yourself wondering if all the energy you were putting into your spiritual life was really getting you anywhere? Did you find yourself wondering whether or not you might actually be better off returning to lay life and using your family wealth to do some good in the world, and at least in that way making some merit?' Sona was taken aback. These were exactly the thoughts that had been going through his mind as he paced up and down.

'Were you not once a fine lute-player, Sona?'

'Indeed I was, Lord.'

'Tell me, when your lute strings were slack did the instrument play well and sound well.'

'No, Lord.'

'And when the lute strings were too tight did the instrument play well and sound well.'

'Certainly not, Lord.'

'But when the lute strings were well tuned, neither too slack nor too tight, did the instrument play well and sound well then.'

'Indeed it did, Lord.'

'It is just the same in the spiritual life, Sona. Too much of the wrong sort of energy leads to agitation and restlessness, and too little energy makes for slackness and dullness. You must look for evenness in your energy, and balance in your spiritual faculties. You can use your experience as a musician to help you achieve this.'

Alone again, Sona steadily applied himself in the way the Buddha had taught him. His feet were no longer cut and blistered, and he soon attained the wisdom of the Enlightened Ones.

Let the silent sage move about in the village as
the bee goes taking honey from the flower
without harming colour or fragrance.

Dhammapada 49

20

BAHIYA OF THE BARK GARMENT

IN A HUT on India's western seashore, there lived a holy man known as Bahiya of the Bark Garment, because his rough clothes were made from bark fibres. He had been living the life of a hermit for many years and was revered and respected by all who knew him. The local villagers met his needs, and he was content.

One day, the thought occurred to him. 'Having lived the holy life like this for all these years, surely I must be among the Enlightened Ones now living in this world.' This thought had barely arisen in Bahiya's mind when a god, who had been a relation of Bahiya's in a former life and who was concerned for his spiritual well-being, came to him and said, 'Bahiya, you are certainly not an Enlightened One, nor are you on the path to Enlightenment, nor are you doing anything that might lead you onto that path.'

This came as a rude shock to Bahiya, but his aspiration was pure and he was perplexed rather than offended or disheartened. He promptly responded with a question: 'If

I am not an Enlightened One, nor on the path to Enlightenment, is there anyone anywhere in this world who is?'

'Far, far to the north,' came the reply, 'in a city called Savatthi, there is an Enlightened One, a Buddha, who teaches the way by which others may realize that goal.'

This exchange roused Bahiya from his complacency. He immediately abandoned the comfortable life he had been enjoying and set off on the long journey north, in search of the city of Savatthi and the Enlightened One who was living there. It was a long journey, and he knew it would take him many weeks, but such was the sense of urgency that now fired Bahiya that he stopped to rest nowhere for more than a single night.

He arrived eventually in Savatthi, and found the Jeta Grove where he was told the Buddha was staying. In the park were many yellow-robed monks, and Bahiya asked where he could find the Buddha. They told him the Buddha was out begging his food, and invited Bahiya to rest and make himself at ease. He would be able to see the Buddha when he returned in an hour or two.

But Bahiya could not wait. The sense of urgency that had driven him all the way from the coast, and that had carried him through the long and difficult journey, grew yet stronger now that he was so near his goal. He hurried into Savatthi, and soon spotted a calm, serene figure whom he recognized instantly as the Buddha, going from house to house on his almsround. Bahiya ran up to him, fell at his feet, and begged the Buddha to teach him.

'Now is not the right time, Bahiya,' replied the Buddha, 'I am in the midst of begging my food.'

'Life is dangerous Lord,' responded Bahiya. 'We cannot know when your life or mine will end. Please teach me now!' Again the Buddha replied that now was not the right time, and again Bahiya put his urgent request. Having been asked for a third time the Buddha responded with a direct and pithy teaching. 'In the seen, only the seen. In the heard, only the heard. In the sensed, only the sensed. In the known, only the known. This is the way you must train yourself Bahiya. When in the seen there is only the seen, in the heard only the heard, in the sensed only the sensed, in the known only the known, then any "you", Bahiya, will not be found either inside or outside of the experience. Here lies the end of suffering.'

These few words were enough to precipitate a profound turning about deep in Bahiya's consciousness. There and then, in that very moment, he gained Enlightenment.

The Buddha, having given this teaching, turned and continued his almsround. As the newly awakened Bahiya went on his way a cow ran into him and killed him. Returning from Savatthi that afternoon with a number of monks, the Buddha saw the body lying by the roadside, where it had been left. Bahiya was unknown in the neighbourhood and no one was in a hurry to take responsibility for a dead wanderer. The Buddha immediately recognized the body as that of the man he had taught only that morning. He told the monks who were with him to take the body and cremate it, and then to build a stupa for the ashes. 'Bahiya of the Bark Garment can be remembered,' he said, 'as one who joined the company of the Enlightened Ones before he died.'

Though one should live a hundred years unethical and unintegrated, better is one single day lived ethically and absorbed (in higher meditative states).

Though one should live a hundred years of evil understanding and unintegrated, better is one single day lived possessed of wisdom and absorbed (in higher meditative states).

Better than a hundred years lived lazily and with inferior energy is one single day lived with energy aroused and fortified.

Dhammapada 110–2

21

CONTRADICTOR

CONTRADICTOR was a brahmin who lived in Savatthi. He was known by that name because he was always picking arguments with people. Whatever anyone said, he always said the opposite. If they said big, he said small. If they said long, he said short. If they said fat, he said thin. Needless to say, he did not have many friends, and often found he had nobody to talk to. One day, hearing that the Buddha was staying near Savatthi, Contradictor (Pachchanika in Pali) said to himself, 'I will go and visit that holy man Gotama, and whatever he says, I will argue the opposite. Let us see what he makes of that! We'll soon find out how holy he really is!'

He set out for the Jeta Grove where he knew the Buddha was often to be found, and he had not long been in the park before he spotted the Buddha walking up and down, slowly and mindfully, in the open air. Contradictor went up to the Buddha, and began to walk alongside him. 'Let's hear a teaching then, monk,' he said. The Buddha stopped walking and slowly turned to face Contradictor. His eyes took him in and he spoke gravely. 'No. There is no teaching for you Contradictor. With your twisted heart so full of anger you will not be able to think clearly or enter into honest discussion. Only a person who has overcome strife and ill will in his heart, and given up all enmity, will be able to recognize the Truth when he hears it.'

These unexpected words caught Contradictor completely off his guard, and for once he was at a loss and could think of nothing to say. He was shaken to the core as, with a shock of recognition, he saw clearly what he had been doing for so many years with his constant arguing. Full of remorse, and determined to change his ways, he opened his heart to the Buddha and listened earnestly to his teaching. That very day he asked to be accepted by the Buddha as a lay disciple.

Do not speak roughly to anyone: those thus spoken to will answer back. Painful indeed is angry talk, (as a result of which) one will experience retribution.

If you (can) silence yourself like a shattered metal plate you have already attained Nirvana: no anger is found in you.

Dhammapada 133–4

22

THE MUSTARD SEED

THERE WAS ONCE a young woman called Kisa, or 'Skinny', Gotami. She came from a poor family which could offer very little to a potential husband in the way of a dowry. However, a husband was eventually found for her, and she went to live with his family, but they looked down on her because of the poor dowry.

Her in-laws behaved harshly towards her and made her work very hard, treating her as little more than an unpaid servant. In time, she gave birth to a son and her life changed. Her child brought her new joy, and she found herself treated with greater respect by her relatives. Unfortunately, while the child was still very young he became sick. The illness grew worse and Kisa Gotami watched desperately as his life faded. Despite all her efforts he died. In her grief she grew hysterical and refused to believe he was dead. She clung to his body and would not let her relatives take it away. Clutching the body she wandered through the village, begging people to give her medicine to cure her son. Some treated her with scorn, while some responded with bewilderment or confused embarrassment. Others tried to reason with her and offered her kindness and consolation. They tried to make her accept the fact that her child was dead, but she would not listen. The only thing she wanted was medicine to make her son better. Eventually, someone told her to go to the Buddha. He was reputed to have all sorts of mysterious powers, and perhaps he would be able to help her. With renewed hope she hurried off to look for him, and finally, bedraggled and tearful, she found herself in his presence, hysterically pleading with him to give her medicine for her child.

The Buddha looked kindly at Kisa Gotami and the dead child in her arms. 'Yes, I can help you,' he said, 'But before I can make the medicine you must bring me one thing. I will need a mustard seed.' Overjoyed, Kisa Gotami was about to rush off. Every home in India had a pot of mustard seed in the kitchen, and soon she would have medicine for her son. 'There is just one condition, though,' the Buddha continued, 'The seed must come from a household in which no one has died.' Not giving this a second thought, the young woman went on her way, hope in her heart.

She called at the first house she came to and asked for a mustard seed. The woman who lived there was happy to give her a seed, but then Kisa Gotami remembered the Buddha's words. 'Has anyone ever died in this household?' she asked. 'Only last month my grandfather died. Please do not remind us.' And so Kisa Gotami went from house to house. Everywhere people were happy to give her a mustard seed, but it was always the same story. Here a wife, there a husband, a brother, sister, mother, father, son, daughter; every household was all too familiar with death. 'The living are few, but the dead are many. Do not remind us of our grief,' she was told, again and again.

Kisa Gotami slowly came to realize that death comes to all, and that she was not alone in her loss. Calm and sobered, she looked at the child in her arms, and was finally able to accept that he was indeed dead. She took his body to the funeral ground, bade him farewell, and returned to the Buddha.

The Buddha welcomed her and asked if she had found the mustard seed he needed to make the medicine. 'The work of the seed is already done,' she declared, and she asked the Buddha to accept her as his disciple and to ordain her as a nun. Later, meditating in the forest, Kisa Gotami gained the perfect release of Enlightenment.

As a great flood carries away a sleeping village, so death bears off the man who, possessed of longing, plucks only the flowers (of existence).

Dhammapada 47

23

MIRACLES

THE BUDDHA was once staying at Nalanda, when a householder called Kevaddha came to him and said, 'Lord, Nalanda is a prosperous and well-populated city, and you already have many disciples here. It would be a good idea if you asked one of your monks to perform a miracle, so that even more of the people of Nalanda would be won over, and everyone would have even greater faith in you.'

The Buddha replied, 'Kevaddha, that is not the way I train my monks, telling them to go and perform miracles just to impress the householders.' Kevaddha, however, really wanted to see a miracle performed, and persisted, determined to persuade the Buddha to have a monk perform a miracle. Again the Buddha refused, and after Kevaddha put his argument forward a third time he said, 'Listen Kevaddha, there are three kinds of miracle I can speak of from my own experience. The first is the miracle of supernormal powers, by which one can emanate many bodies, pass through walls, walk on water, and even visit the realms of the gods. The second is the miracle of reading others' minds. And the third is the miracle of teaching.

'If either of these first two miracles is displayed just to impress people, it is impossible to distinguish it from the art of the magician, and performed in that way it is of no spiritual value whatsoever. I despise, and will have nothing to do with, such cheap miracle-making.

'The miracle of teaching comes about when a holy man offers people guidance as to how best to live. When a Buddha appears in the world and through his own direct knowledge and vision sees into the true nature of things, and when that Buddha teaches the way so that the disciple who applies himself also attains that same knowledge and vision, that is a true miracle. Indeed, Kevaddha, that is the only real miracle.' The Buddha then told Kevaddha the story of a monk who was able to perform the first two miracles, but whose powers did not in the end benefit him in his search for truth:

There was once a monk who had a burning question to which he sought an answer. The question was, 'Where do the four great elements of earth, water, fire, and air come to an end completely, so that there is nothing left of any of them?' Entering a deep concentration, the way to the realm of the gods opened up before him, and this monk ascended to the realm of the four great kings. Thinking he would find an answer there, he put his question to the gods.

'We don't know,' replied the gods, 'but surely the four great kings will know. Go and ask them.' The four great kings, however, on being questioned, had no answer either, and they in turn suggested the monk ask the higher gods of the Tavitimsa Heaven. He travelled up to this lofty realm, but there too the gods were unable to give him an answer. In this way the monk passed higher and higher through the many heavens, until he eventually came to the Brahma Heaven, the heaven of the very highest gods.

There the monk again put his question, and again he was disappointed. 'We don't know the answer to that question, monk,' they replied, 'but there is Brahmá, great Brahma, unsurpassed great being, maker and creator, all-seeing, all-powerful, master of all who are and can ever be, who is far greater than us. He surely will be able to answer your question.'

'Where is the great Brahma to be found, friends?'

'He is not here at present, and it is not for us to know the comings and goings of the great Brahma. But we can tell when he is about to arrive, for a great light shines out just before he appears.'

The monk waited, and before long he saw a great light, followed by the appearance of Brahma. The monk approached the great god and asked his question:

'Where do the four great elements of earth, water, fire, and air come to an end completely, so that there is nothing left of any of them?'

'I am great Brahma, unsurpassed great being, maker and creator, all-seeing, all-powerful, master of all who are and can ever be.'

Baffled by this response, but undaunted, the monk said, 'Friend, that was not what I asked. What I want to know is, where do the four great elements of earth, water, fire, and air cease completely, so that there is nothing left of any of them?'

Again Brahma responded with, 'I am great Brahma, unsurpassed great being, maker and creator, all-seeing, all-powerful, master of all who are and can ever be.'

'Friend, that is not what I asked you.'

The monk patiently put his question again. Brahma now took him by the arm and led him aside. 'The gods here think I know everything, so I cannot answer in their presence. I don't know where the four elements completely come to an end. You had better go back and ask the Buddha, and listen very carefully to what he has to say.'

So the monk came back down from the heavens, and asked the Buddha his question. 'Your question is wrongly worded, monk,' the Buddha replied. 'The correct question is, "Where do earth, water, fire, and air find no footing?" And the answer is: where consciousness is signless, limitless, and luminous.

Kevaddha was left to reflect on this story, and no longer pestered the Buddha to get his disciples to perform miracles. With his faith in the Buddha confirmed and strengthened, Kevaddha soon gained the insight that made him irreversible on the path to Enlightenment.

Those who take the unreal for the real, and who in the real see the unreal, they, wandering in the sphere of wrong thought, will not attain the real.

Those who have known the real as the real, and the unreal as the unreal, they, moving in the sphere of right thought, will attain the real.

Dhammapada 11–12

24

ANANDA

FROM TIME TO TIME the Buddha would go off alone to enjoy the peace and solitude of the forest, but as his fame spread and the number of his followers grew, more and more people came to seek him out, wishing to be in his presence and to hear him teach.

The Buddha usually had an attendant whose job was to look after his needs and deal with various requests, but not all these attendants proved very reliable. One such was the youthful Meghiya, who left the Buddha in order to meditate in a beautiful mango grove that caught his eye. Another time, the Buddha was travelling in Kosala with a monk called Nagasamala as his attendant. They came to a fork in the highway, and Nagasamala insisted they take one road while the Buddha was clear they should take the other. In the end, Nagasamala just put the Buddha's robe and bowl down in the road and strode off the way he wanted to go. He had not travelled very far, however, when he was set upon by robbers, who beat him and kicked him, breaking his bowl and ripping his robe to shreds. He returned and followed the same road as the Buddha, and when he caught up with him – feeling rather sorry for himself – he related what had befallen him.

After twenty years of such experiences the Buddha decided he had had enough. Calling an assembly of the monks together, he declared, 'I have had many attendants over the years, but none of them has done the job perfectly. Time and again selfishness and wilfulness have come into play. I am fifty-five years old now, and I need a reliable and trustworthy attendant.' One by one the most senior monks offered their services, but one by one the Buddha turned them down. Then they all looked at Ananda who had so far remained silent out of modesty.

'The Buddha surely knows who will be most suitable,' Ananda said, making it clear that if he was asked he would very happy to serve him. The Buddha said he would be very happy with Ananda as his attendant, and that he was indeed the one best suited to the job.

Before he accepted the position, however, Ananda asked the Buddha to agree to eight conditions. He asked the Buddha not to pass on to him gifts of robes, food, or dwellings, and not automatically to include him in invitations for meals. These four conditions were intended to ensure that no one could say of Ananda that he took on the job of the Buddha's attendant for personal gain.

He asked to be allowed to pass invitations made to him on to the Buddha. He asked that if people came from far away to see the Buddha, he would have the privilege of leading them into his presence. He asked that if he ever had any doubts or questions about the Buddha's teaching, he could have them cleared up at any time. Finally, he asked that if the Buddha delivered any teachings in his absence, they would be repeated to him later. These last four conditions were intended to ensure his continued progress on the path while he fulfilled his duties to the Buddha. The last condition, as well as serving Ananda's own spiritual progress, was also to prove of great benefit to the whole community. With his phenomenal memory, Ananda was to be one of the great repositories and guardians of the Buddha's teaching.

The Buddha happily agreed to these conditions, and Ananda became his constant companion for the remaining twenty-five years of his life, looking to the Buddha's needs and wishes with constant kindness and care. He would bring the Buddha water to wash and twigs to clean his teeth, he would arrange his seat and massage his back for him, fan him, mend his robes, and obtain medicine when he was sick. As well as taking care of the Buddha's everyday needs he acted as a channel of communication between the Buddha and his disciples, monk and lay, fulfilling his duties with great tact and kindness, so that he became loved and respected by all.

A man is not spiritually mature (or: learned) merely because he talks a lot. He is said to be spiritually mature who is secure (in himself), friendly, and without fear.

Dhammapada 258

25

A SICK MONK

ONE DAY the Buddha and Ananda were visiting the monks' lodgings when they came across a monk who was sick with dysentery. He had collapsed and lay helpless on the floor, covered in his own urine and excrement. Concerned to see one of his disciples in such a miserable state, the Buddha went over to the monk and asked him what was wrong.

'I have dysentery, Lord.'

'But isn't anyone looking after you?'

'No, Lord.'

'But why are you not cared for by the other monks?'

'I am of no use to them, Lord. That is why they do not look after me.'

The Buddha turned to Ananda and asked him to fetch warm water so that they could wash the monk. When Ananda returned with the water they washed him, then they lifted him on to his bed, the Buddha taking his head and Ananda his feet. Having made sure the monk was comfortable and had all he needed, they left him. The Buddha then summoned all the monks living in that neighbourhood to a meeting.

'Monks are you aware there is a sick monk in that hut over there?' he asked.

'We are, Lord.'

'What is wrong with him?'

'He has dysentery, Lord.'

'Is anyone looking after him?'

'No, Lord.'

'Why are other monks not looking after him?'

'Because he is of no use to us, Lord.'

'Monks, you have given up everything to follow the spiritual life. You no longer have parents or relatives to look after you. If you do not look after one another who will look after you? Just as you would look after me, your teacher, in the same way you must take care of one of your brothers when he is sick. If a sick monk has a preceptor, that preceptor should look after him until he is well again. If he has a teacher, that teacher should look after him. Or it could be someone whom he lives with, one of his pupils, or someone who shares the same preceptor or teacher. If there is no one obvious to take care of a sick monk, then the responsibility falls to the whole community. You must regard this as a firm rule of training that cannot be ignored or broken. You must take care of one another!'

One should pay no heed to the faults of others, what they have done and not done. Rather should one consider the things that one has oneself done and not done.

Like a beautiful flower, brightly coloured but without scent, even so useless is the well-uttered speech of one who does not act accordingly.

Like a beautiful flower, brightly coloured and scented, even so useful is the well-uttered speech of one who acts accordingly.

Dhammapada 50–2

26

THE ALAVI YAKSHA

THE KING OF ALAVI, one of the many small kingdoms of northern India, regularly went out hunting with his army in order to keep it in training. One day, the animal they were hunting escaped past the king, who was lying in wait for it, and according to custom it was then his duty to hunt it down. After a chase that led him deep into the jungle he finally caught and killed it. He was returning home very late, exhausted, when he passed under a banyan tree in which a yaksha had his palace. This yaksha had been granted permission by the king of the yakshas to eat anyone who came within the shadow of the tree, and he was delighted to see such a tasty morsel arrive. He seized the king and told him of his intention to eat him. The king was horrified at the thought of becoming a yaksha's dinner, and sought desperately to persuade the creature to free him. This he achieved, but only at a price. In return for his own life he promised to provide the yaksha with a regular meal in the form of a human being and a bowl of food.

At first, the criminals of Alavi were fed to the yaksha, and this seemed a reasonable arrangement. But after a time there were no criminals left, so every family was ordered to take it in turns to provide a child to give to the yaksha. Families began to leave the city, and eventually, after twelve years, the only child left was the king's own son. The king could not break his promise so, although it caused him great pain, he ordered the boy to be dressed in his finest clothes and taken to the yaksha.

Fortunately, the Buddha intervened. He was wandering in the region and heard the story of the yaksha. The Buddha went to the yaksha's palace in the banyan tree and asked to see him, but he was told that the yaksha was away at a gathering of yakshas in the Himalayas. The Buddha insisted on waiting and persuaded the door-keeper to let him in, shrugging off his warnings that the yaksha would certainly eat him if he came home and found him there. He sat himself on the yaksha's throne, and while he was waiting he taught the yaksha's womenfolk. Two other yakshas were flying through the air on their way to the conference, and finding they could not fly over the spot where the Buddha was seated, they descended to discover what was going on. They spoke with the Buddha and paid him their respects before continuing to the Himalayas.

When the Alavi yaksha heard that a monk had installed himself in his palace and was seated upon his throne he became very angry and set off home in a great hurry. On his arrival, the yaksha set to work with his supernatural powers to eject the Buddha from his throne. When every effort failed, he tried another tactic. He asked the Buddha to leave the palace, and, to his great astonishment, the Buddha did so. To test how far he could get this monk to comply with his will, the yaksha then asked the Buddha to come back in again, which he did. Enjoying the power of these simple commands, the yaksha repeated the exercise three times, but on his fourth attempt the Buddha refused to re-enter the building. The yaksha questioned the Buddha, hoping to regain power over him, but the Buddha's answers surprised him with their wisdom, and gradually his heart was opened to the truth. Letting go of his desire for power over the Buddha, the yaksha was himself won over and asked to become a disciple. That very night, knowledge and vision of things as they really are arose in him.

The next morning a sad procession came to the yaksha's palace, as the king of Alavi's servants brought the young prince to be sacrificed. The reformed yaksha was ashamed and embarrassed at this reminder of his cruel past, and promptly gave the boy to the Buddha, who blessed him and gave him back to the royal messengers so that he might be returned to his father. The prince was henceforth known as Hatthaka, or 'he who was handed on'.

When the citizens of Alavi heard that the yaksha had reformed and become a disciple of the Buddha, they were very happy and relieved. They built the yaksha a special house in a beautiful spot, and regularly made him offerings of flowers, perfumes, and other fine things. This place was known as the Alavi shrine, and became a favourite resting place for the Buddha on his travels.

The prince Hatthaka, when he grew up, became one of the Buddha's leading lay disciples, and he soon had many disciples of his own. Once, while he was staying at the Alavi shrine, the Buddha spoke in praise of Hatthaka, listing seven marvellous and wonderful qualities that Hatthaka possessed. These were faith, virtue, conscientiousness, not wanting to let down his teacher, being a good listener, generosity, and wisdom. One of the monks present reported the Buddha's praise to Hatthaka, whose first response was that he hoped only monks were present when the Buddha spoke in praise of him, and none of the lay disciples. Hearing of this, the Buddha added an eighth quality to the list: modesty.

On another occasion when the Buddha was staying at Alavi, Hatthaka came to him with 500 lay disciples, all with considerable spiritual attainments.

'You have a very large following, Hatthaka,' the Buddha commented, 'How do you manage to attract so many followers?'

'I apply the four means that you taught for creating sympathy between people. For the benefit of those who will respond to generosity, I practise generosity. For those who will respond to kindly speech, I practise kindly speech. For the benefit of those who will respond to kindly action, I practise kindly action, and for the benefit of those who will respond to being treated as equals, I practise impartiality. It is in this way that I attract people and have thus created this community of disciples.'

The Buddha was pleased with what he heard. He taught Hatthaka and his disciples, and later, when they had departed, he again spoke to the monks in praise of Hatthaka.

Whosoever is energetic, recollected, pure in conduct, considerate, self-restrained, of righteous life, and mindful, the glory of such a one waxes exceedingly.

By means of energy, mindfulness, self-restraint, and control, let the man of understanding make (for himself) an island that no flood can overwhelm.

Out of their evil understanding the spiritually immature abandon themselves to unmindfulness. The man of understanding guards mindfulness as his chief treasure.

Dhammapada 24–6

27

A SNEEZE

THE RULES of the monastic community emerged in response to specific incidents that prompted the Buddha to give instructions as to how he expected his followers to behave. The following story tells of one such incident, and illustrates very well both the clarity and the pragmatism with which the Buddha dealt with various situations.

Once, while teaching a large number of monks, the Buddha happened to sneeze. Immediately there was a chorus of monks saying, 'Long life to you, Lord, long life to you,' as was customary when somebody sneezed. The noise of this response went on for some moments, and interrupted the flow of the discourse.

'Monks,' said the Buddha, 'When you say "Long life to you" to someone who sneezes, does it really make any difference to them? Is it really a matter of life and death?'

'Of course not, Lord.'

'Then I want you to stop saying "Long life to you" whenever anyone sneezes. That is a rule from now on.'

Soon after this incident one of the monks happened to sneeze while out in the village and a villager responded with the customary 'Long life to you.' The monks who were present were embarrassed, and instead of making the usual polite response of 'May you live long too' they remained silent. The affronted villager talked of this incident and soon people began to complain, saying the followers of the Buddha were very rude, for ignoring anyone who wished them long life after they had sneezed.

This concerned the monks and they reported it back to the Buddha, who proposed a compromise. 'All right monks,' he said, 'Ordinary folk are used to their superstitions and there is no point in giving offence. If they say "Long life to you" when you sneeze, you may make the customary response of "May you live long too," but among ourselves we can forget such superstitions.'

(The mind) is frivolous and difficult to control, alighting on whatever it pleases. It is good to tame the mind. A tamed mind brings happiness.

The mind is extremely subtle and difficult to grasp, alighting on whatever it pleases. Let the man of understanding keep watch over the mind. A guarded mind brings happiness.

Dhammapada 35–6

28

AN INSULTING BRAHMIN

AT A TIME when the Buddha was staying at Veranja with a large number of his followers, a brahmin called Udaya, who had heard many criticisms of the Buddha from his fellow brahmins, came to visit him. After polite greetings had been exchanged, the brahmin spoke, and it soon became clear that he had come to put the Buddha in his place.

'Master Gotama, I have heard it said that you do not pay proper respect to old and learned brahmins, and I have seen for myself that this is the case. This is not the way to behave, Master Gotama.'

The Buddha was not slow to respond.

'Brahmin, there is no one in the whole world who is worthy of the respect of an Enlightened One. If a Buddha were to pay deference to anyone their head would probably split wide open!'

'Master Gotama has no taste!' came the retort.

'Well, there is a sense in which it could be said I have no taste, for I no longer have any taste for the world of the senses. But that is surely not what you mean?'

'Master Gotama has no sense of values!'

'There is a sense in which it could be said I have no sense of values, for I attach no value to the world of the senses. But that is surely not what you mean.'

'Master Gotama teaches passivity!'

'There is a sense in which you could say I teach passivity, for I teach that one must be passive in the face of provocation or temptation and not go along with evil actions of body, speech, or mind. But that is surely not what you mean?'

'Master Gotama teaches nihilism!'

'There is a sense in which you could say I teach nihilism, for I teach the annihilation of greed, hatred, and delusion. But that is surely not what you mean?'

'Master Gotama teaches rejection!'

'There is a sense in which you could say I teach rejection, for I teach the rejection of all evil actions of body, speech, and mind. But that is surely not what you mean?'

'Master Gotama teaches destruction!'

'There is a sense in which you could say I teach destruction, for I teach the destruction of greed, hatred, and delusion. But that is surely not what you mean?'

'Master Gotama teaches mortification!'

'There is a sense in which I teach mortification, for I teach the mortification of all actions rooted in greed, hatred, and delusion. But that is surely not what you mean?'

'Master Gotama rejects rebirth!'

'There is a sense in which I reject rebirth, for having completely freed myself from all defilements I will never again come to birth in a womb. But that is surely not what you mean?'

At last, the brahmin's anger and ill will was spent, and he had no more insults to throw at the Buddha. Seeing this, the Buddha asked him a question.

'Brahmin, tell me, if a hen had carefully incubated a clutch of eggs, and a chick was to break out of one of those eggs before all the others, using its beak to get through the shell, would you call that chick the oldest or the youngest?'

'The oldest, Master Gotama.'

'In just this way brahmin, in this world encased in a shell of ignorance, I was the first to break through the shell, so I can truly be called the elder brother to the world.'

The Buddha went on to describe the unfoldment of his Enlightenment as being like breaking through successive shells, leading eventually to the attainment of complete liberation. By the time the Buddha had finished, the brahmin had been completely won over, and joyfully declared, 'Master Gotama is indeed the elder brother to the world. Master Gotama is indeed the best of men. It is wonderful, Master Gotama, wonderful. It is just as if something had been set upright that had been overturned; as if something had been uncovered that was long hidden; as though a lamp had been brought into a dark room so that all may see clearly. Master Gotama has made the Truth very clear to me. I go for refuge to Master Gotama, to his teaching, and to his community from this day on and for the rest of my life.'

Experiences are preceded by mind, led by mind, and produced by mind. If one speaks or acts with an impure mind, suffering follows even as the cartwheel follows the hoof of the ox (drawing the cart).

Experiences are preceded by mind, led by mind, and produced by mind. If one speaks or acts with a pure mind, happiness follows like his shadow.

Dhammapada 1–2

29

A KING'S VISIT

THE BUDDHA was once staying at Rajagaha, in the mango grove of Jivaka the royal doctor, together with some 1,250 monks. It was a full-moon night, and King Ajatasattu of Magadha was sitting on the roof of his palace surrounded by his courtiers. The king had a troubled conscience, for he had plotted against his father, the former King Bimbisara, who had been a friend and faithful disciple of the Buddha's. When the old king had found out about the plot he had readily given the throne over to Ajatasattu, but even so, the fearful and untrusting prince had had his father imprisoned and eventually starved him to death.

'This is a beautiful full-moon night,' declared Ajatasattu, 'an auspicious night for visiting some holy man who might bring me some peace of mind.'

One by one, his ministers and advisers suggested various holy men, but the king received each suggestion with a stony silence. He had visited them all, questioned them all, and found every one of them lacking. No more suggestions were forthcoming, and Ajatasattu turned to his doctor, Jivaka.

'Friend Jivaka, why do you not say anything?'

Jivaka now spoke. 'There is Gotama, the Buddha, sir. He is staying in my mango grove with 1,250 monks. If you were to visit him, perhaps he would help you to find some peace of mind.'

Ajatasattu approved of the suggestion. 'Good, let us visit him Jivaka. Have my elephants made ready.'

The king did not set out alone. As well as the royal elephant on which he rode with Jivaka, there were 500 elephants for his wives and a great company of soldiers and torch-bearers. The royal procession slowly wound its way out of the city and into the countryside, towards Jivaka's secluded mango grove. As they approached the mango grove the air seemed to vibrate with a tremendous silence, and Ajatasattu grew afraid and his hair stood on end.

'Jivaka, are you betraying me?' he asked, 'Are you leading me into a trap laid by my enemies? You said the Buddha was here with 1,250 monks. Yet we do not hear a single voice, cough, or sneeze. How is that so?'

'Your Majesty, you need not be afraid. I would never betray you or give you into the hands of your enemies. Do you see that light over there? That is where the Buddha sits with his monks. Let us go to him.'

Having ridden as far as they could, Jivaka and Ajatasattu climbed down from the elephant and entered the mango grove. A remarkable sight awaited them. In a small pavilion, his back against a pillar, sat the Buddha. All around him, in total silence, like a calm lake, sat hundreds of meditating monks.

'If only my son could know calm and peace like this!' said Ajatasattu, deeply moved.

The king respectfully approached the Buddha and sat down beside him. He asked many questions, and the Buddha responded with spiritual teachings. They sat together for a long time, and Ajatasattu was much affected by the discussion. He asked to be accepted as a lay disciple of the Buddha and confessed to him the terrible wrong he had done in killing his father.

The Buddha received his confession and accepted him as a disciple, and after formal farewells had been made, they parted. When the king had gone, the Buddha declared that Ajatasattu's fate was sealed. His deeds would soon catch up with him. But had he not had the death of his father on his conscience, he could have awakened to the truth that very night and been firmly established on the path to Enlightenment.

As long as it bears no fruit, so long the evildoer sees the evil (he has done) as good. When it bears fruit (in the form of suffering) he recognizes it as evil.

As long as it bears no fruit, so long the good man sees (the good he has done) as evil. When it bears fruit (in the form of happiness), then he recognizes it as good.

Dhammapada 119–20

30

UGGA

UGGA OF HATTHIGAMA was one of the Buddha's leading lay disciples. He was a wealthy banker and became well known for his generosity and care in serving the order of monks. He first met the Buddha in most inauspicious circumstances. The Buddha was visiting Hatthigama and staying in a park just outside the city. One day, not realizing the Buddha was there, Ugga came to the park with a party of friends and dancing girls. He had been drinking and feasting for seven days and was drunk and dishevelled. Arriving in a clearing, Ugga was suddenly confronted with the serene and beautiful figure of the Buddha sitting in contemplation beneath a tree. The other revellers were caught between the temptation to laugh at him and the uncomfortable desire to slink off elsewhere and continue their partying, but the sight of the Buddha had a dramatic effect on Ugga. He recognized the drunken and dissipated state he was in, and was seized with shame. Instantly his drunkenness disappeared and his mind became clear.

Leaving his companions, Ugga approached the Buddha and paid his respects. The Buddha invited Ugga to sit beside him, and soon the two men were deep in conversation. The Buddha found his visitor to be open and receptive, and ready to receive his teaching, so he led him step by step into a deeper understanding of the true nature of things. Ugga's spiritual vision unfolded and became so profound that he would never again need to undergo a human birth. That very day he became a 'non-returner', with the confidence that after death he would move swiftly towards Enlightenment. Turning away from his previous way of life, Ugga became a devoted and generous disciple of the Buddha.

On a visit to Hatthigama some years later the Buddha praised Ugga's eight special and wonderful qualities, though he did not specify what they were. A monk who had heard this approached Ugga and asked him what the qualities might be that the Buddha had spoken of so highly. Ugga replied that he could not say what the Buddha had in mind, but he could tell the monk about eight wonderful things that had happened to him.

'Firstly, when I first saw the Buddha in the park many years ago, my drunkenness left me completely and instantaneously. I paid my respects to the Buddha and he taught me about generosity and ethics and laid out for me the whole spiritual path.

'Secondly, when the Buddha saw my mind was ready, he taught me about suffering, its cause, its cessation, and the way leading to its cessation. I quickly grasped the profound significance of this teaching, and awoke to the true nature of things.

'Thirdly, at that time I had four young and beautiful wives. Having broken the fetter of sensual desire, and remaining a householder, I adopted a life of celibacy and devotion to the Buddha's teachings. I offered my wives a choice. They could join me in my new life, or, if they preferred, I would free them from their marriage obligations and find them another husband. The three younger wives chose to follow me, but the eldest asked to be freed. I gave her in marriage to the man of her choice, and in doing this I experienced no feelings of jealousy.

'Fourthly, I am able to share my considerable wealth with good and noble men, by supporting the Buddha and his disciples.

'Fifthly, whenever I wait upon a monk, I do so wholeheartedly. If the monk preaches, I listen earnestly. If the monk does not preach, then I myself teach the doctrine.

'Sixthly, gods often come and tell me of the different qualities and attainments of particular monks, encouraging me to feed those who are most deserving and thereby gain the most merit for myself. But I take no notice of such recommendations, and serve all equally.

'Seventhly, I take no pride in the fact that gods come and speak with me in this fashion.

'Finally, I have no fear of death, for the Buddha has assured me I will never need to return to this or any lower world.'

The monk later described this conversation to the Buddha, who commented that Ugga had listed exactly the qualities he had had in mind.

One is indeed one's own saviour (or: protector). What other saviour should there be? With oneself well-controlled, one finds a saviour hard to find.

The evil done by oneself, born of oneself, produced by oneself, destroys the man of evil understanding as a diamond pulverizes a piece of rock crystal.

Easily done are things which are bad and not beneficial to oneself. What is (both) beneficial and good, that is exceedingly difficult to do.

Dhammapada 160–1, 163

31

THE STABILITY OF THE ORDER

WHEN THE BUDDHA reached the age of eighty, he entered what was to be the last year of his life. He was staying with Ananda, his cousin and constant companion of the last twenty-five years, at the Vulture's Peak just outside the city of Rajagaha. From this vantage point they could look down over the jungle and fields and see the houses and palaces of the populous city gleaming in the valley.

In his palace at Rajagaha, King Ajatasattu sat plotting with his minister Vassakara. He wanted to attack the neighbouring Vajjian republic and annexe it to his kingdom of Magadha. The king sent Vassakara to the Buddha with careful instructions:

'Go to the Buddha, Vassakara. Pay your respects, and greet him in my name. Then tell him that King Ajatasattu plans to attack the Vajjians, and to bring them to destruction and ruin. Listen very carefully to what he has to say in reply, for a Buddha never lies. Then come back and tell me.'

Vassakara had a royal chariot made ready, and rode in it as far as he could, to the foot of the Vulture's Peak. There he dismounted and continued on foot up the steep mountainside to where the Buddha was staying. Arriving at the summit, he greeted the Buddha, paid his respects, and delivered Ajatasattu's message. Ananda was standing behind the Buddha, fanning him, and the Buddha turned and spoke to him.

'Ananda, do you know if the Vajjians hold frequent and well attended assemblies?'

'I have heard that they do, Lord.'

'As long as they continue to do this, Ananda, we can expect them to prosper and not to decline. Do you know if they assemble in harmony, do their business in harmony and rise in harmony?'

'I have heard that they do, Lord.'

'So long as they do this, we can expect them to prosper and not decline.'

The Buddha continued in the same vein:

'Ananda, do you know if the Vajjians live according to their traditional laws, without forever changing them and bringing in new laws? Do they honour and respect their elders and take good notice of their advice and experience? Do they live peaceably, without abducting and raping the women and girls of their own and neighbouring clans? Do they venerate the traditional Vajjian shrines? Do they welcome and take good care of Enlightened Ones and their followers who enter Vajjian territory?'

To each question, Ananda replied, 'I have heard they do, Lord.' And following each such response the Buddha concluded that as long as they continued to live in this way, the Vajjians would remain strong and prosper.

Turning to Vassakara, the Buddha told him that he had himself, while staying at Vesali, taught the Vajjians these seven rules of conduct that would prevent their decline, and he had assured them that as long as they remembered them, practised them, and taught them, the Vajjians would be prosperous and strong, and not fall into decline.

Vassakara was pleased with what he heard and reached for himself the following conclusion: 'As long as the Vajjians practise even one of these things, never mind all seven, they will remain strong. King Ajatasattu will never get the better of them by fighting. The only way he will ever defeat such a people is if he manages to buy some of them over and create divisions between them.' Having uttered this remark, he paid his respects to the Buddha and returned to the palace.

For a while the Buddha remained deep in thought. Then he turned to Ananda and asked him to summon all the monks living in the area to a meeting. He knew his own death would not be long in coming, and the encounter with Ajatasattu's minister had set him thinking about the future of his order of monks. When the monks were assembled the Buddha took his seat and spoke to them.

'Monks, I want you to pay close attention and listen very carefully to what I have to say. I am going to teach you seven things that will ensure this community continues to prosper for a long time and does not fall into decline.

'As long as the monks come together frequently and in large numbers, the community will continue to prosper and not decline. As long as they come together in harmony, do their business in harmony, and depart in harmony, the community will continue to prosper and not decline. As long as the monks maintain the institutions and training rules we have set up, and are not forever changing things round and making innovations, the community will continue to prosper and not decline. As long as the monks honour and respect those who set out on the path long ago and who are deeply experienced in the life of the order, and follow their guidance, the community will continue to prosper and not decline. As long as the monks do not fall under the power of craving, the community will continue to prosper and not decline. As long as there are monks who lead the simple forest life, the community will continue to prosper and not decline. As long as the monks maintain clear awareness, so that further good companions in the holy life are attracted to join them, and those who have already chosen this life are able to live happily together, the community will continue to prosper and not decline. For as long as these seven things are done by all of you, so long will our community continue to prosper and not decline.'

That was not all. The Buddha continued, setting out seven further conditions that would prevent the decline of the community and ensure its future prosperity.

'As long as the monks avoid finding pleasure and satisfaction in busyness and constant activity, gossiping and useless chatter, laziness and sleep, socializing, as long as they do not full under the spell of evil desires, or evil friends who might lead them astray, and as long as the monks do not get side-tracked by the attainment of merely mundane powers and stop half-way along the spiritual path, the community will continue to flourish and not decline.'

The more he spoke, the more thoughts came to the Buddha, as he gave expression to his concern for the future of the order he had founded. He urged his monks to devote themselves to a wholehearted concern for the harmony and collective life of the community and to a single-minded pursuit of the highest goal.

Irrigators draw off waters; fletchers straighten arrows; carpenters shape wood; the spiritually mature discipline themselves.

As a solid rock cannot be shaken by the wind, so the spiritually mature person is unmoved by praise or blame.

Hearing the Truth of Things, the spiritually mature win insight like a deep lake (suddenly) becoming clear and undisturbed.

Dhammapada 80–2

32

THE LAST DAYS

THE BUDDHA spent his last rainy season with Ananda near a small village called Beluva, not far from Vesali, where he became very ill with dysentery. His body was racked with dreadful pains and he came close to death, but wishing to say a proper farewell to his disciples the Buddha suppressed the sickness by a tremendous act of will and slowly began to recover. When at length he was able to get up from his bed and sit outside in the sun for a while, Ananda breathed a sigh of relief. He had seen how close to death the Buddha had come and had been afraid this was the end. He had reassured himself with the thought that surely his master would not die without giving final instructions to the community of disciples. When he told the Buddha his thoughts, the Buddha gently chided him.

'But Ananda, what more does the community expect of me? I have taught you all I know. There are no hidden teachings. There is no closed fist, there are no secrets still waiting to be revealed. I am old, and this body of mine is like an old cart, held together with bits of string and soon to fall apart. Only when I withdraw my mind completely from the body am I ever free of pain and discomfort. The time has come when each of you must become an island, a refuge to himself, and no longer rely on me. You must take the Truth as your refuge, and that alone, and devote yourself wholeheartedly to realizing it for yourself.'

When the Buddha was strong enough, he and Ananda set out together on a final tour. Wherever he went, the disciples in the neighbourhood would rapidly pass the word around, and people would flock to see him. Though frail, the Buddha again and again gave of himself. He answered questions about the spiritual life, and once more urged and inspired them to make the utmost effort.

The Buddha and Ananda travelled on, from village to village, town to town, until they came to a place called Pava. Here the Buddha was given a meal by one of his disciples, a goldsmith named Chunda. His dysentery returned and he realized his time had come. He and Ananda continued their journey, but the Buddha was very ill and often in great pain. Despite this, with his customary kindness and concern, the Buddha had a message sent back to Chunda with assurance that he need feel no guilt or remorse over the meal that had brought on this final illness. On the contrary, it was an act of very great merit to have provided a Buddha with his final meal.

They had to make frequent stops, and while resting quietly under a tree the Buddha was approached by a man called Pukussa, a disciple of Alara Kalama, the teacher with whom the young Siddhattha Gotama had himself first trained some fifty years earlier. They conversed and, as he heard the Buddha's words, Pukussa's heart opened and he asked to be accepted as a disciple. Pukussa had with him some fine golden cloth, and asked if he might have it made into robes for the Buddha and Ananda. The Buddha agreed, and the robes were duly made and brought to them. When the splendid material was draped over the Buddha's shoulders, however, it appeared very dull against the beautiful radiance of his golden skin. Ananda remarked on this, and the Buddha told him there were just two occasions on which a Buddha's skin assumes such beautiful clarity and radiance. The first was on the eve of his Enlightenment, and the second just before his death. This was sad news indeed for the faithful Ananda, who dreaded the loss of his teacher.

The Buddha and Ananda continued their travels and eventually came to a pleasant grove of sal trees not far from the town of Kusinara. Between two of the trees was a stone couch upon which the Buddha lay down on his side and made ready to die. The sal trees broke into unseasonable blossoms that showered gently down on the Buddha. Ananda did all he could to see that the Buddha was comfortable and that his needs were met. As the word spread that their master's last hours had come, other disciples gathered in the sal grove. After a while the Buddha looked up and noticed that Ananda was no longer there. On enquiring where he had gone, he was told that he was nearby, leaning on a doorpost, weeping and saying, 'I have still so much to learn, and my teacher who is so kind will soon be gone!'

The Buddha sent for Ananda, and spoke gently to him. 'Come, Ananda, don't weep. Surely you must understand by now that we have to be separated from all we love. How could anything which comes into being not also have an end? For a long time you have unstintingly served me with great love and kindness. You have made great merit Ananda. Just put in the effort and you will soon gain Enlightenment.'

Then the Buddha turned and spoke to the other monks, rejoicing in Ananda's many good qualities. As evening fell, he asked Ananda to go into Kusinara and tell the townsfolk that the Buddha would die in the sal grove that very night. Ananda should invite them to pay him their respects, thus allowing them for one last time the benefit of being in the presence of his wisdom and compassion. The people of Kusinara came in great crowds, many of them weeping and greatly distressed by the news. There were so many of them that Ananda asked them to arrange themselves in family groups, and he presented each group in turn to the Buddha.

There also came a wandering holy man called Subhadda, who happened to be passing through Kusinara. He had heard the news that the Buddha was dying, and saw that this was his last opportunity to receive a teaching from him. He approached Ananda and asked if he might speak with the Buddha.

'You have come too late friend. The Buddha is very tired. Don't trouble him now.' Deeply disappointed, Subhadda tried again, but Ananda was insistent in his refusal. Subhadda had left it too late, he explained again; the Buddha was dying and now was not the time to trouble him. Weak as he was, the Buddha overheard their conversation and he called to Ananda to let Subhadda come to him.

Subhadda stepped towards the Buddha and paid his respects. He began by asking which of the other well-known teachers of the day had real insight and which did not, but the Buddha had no time for such questions. He communicated directly the heart of his own teaching and Subhadda's response was immediate and wholehearted. He asked the Buddha to accept him into his order of monks. Wanderers who had followed other teachers were usually subject to a probation period of four months before being ordained. When he was told this, Subhadda declared he would be happy to wait four years, but the Buddha saw clearly that there would be no wavering in his commitment, and told Ananda to ordain him there and then.

The night drew on, and by the early hours of the morning a great company of monks had assembled in the sal grove. The Buddha addressed his followers for the last time. 'If any of you have any doubts or questions, speak up now. Do not regret later that you were in the presence of the Buddha and did not ask.' Three times he gave this invitation, and each time they all remained silent. In order to be quite certain that no monk missed his opportunity, he said, 'Monks, if any of you is afraid to speak because you are in awe of me, then speak to a friend and let him ask for you.' Still the company remained silent. Confident that he had done all he could for his disciples, the Buddha now uttered his last words: 'Impermanent are all compounded things. With mindfulness, strive on.'

Then, entering a deep meditation, the Buddha died.

The not doing of anything evil, undertaking to do what is (ethically) skilful, (and) complete purification of the mind – this is the ordinance of the Enlightened Ones.

Dhammapada 183

LIST OF PALI REFERENCES

by chapter number

1 *Majjhima-Nikaya* 26; *Sutta Nipata* iii.11
2 *Majjhima-Nikaya* 26 and 36
3 *Majjhima-Nikaya* 26 and 36
4 *Majjhima-Nikaya* 26; *Vinaya Mahavagga* 1
5 *Vinaya Mahavagga* 1
6 *Vinaya Mahavagga* 1
7 *Udana* iii.2
8 *Majjhima-Nikaya* 61
9 *Vinaya Cullavagga* 7
10 *Vinaya Cullavagga* 6
11 *Vinaya Mahavagga* 10
12 *Majjhima-Nikaya* 128
13 *Samyutta-Nikaya* i.172–3
14 *Udana* iv.1
15 *Majjhima-Nikaya* 86
16 *Majjhima-Nikaya* 95
17 *Samyutta-Nikaya* i.237–8
18 *Samyutta-Nikaya* i.177–8

19 *Vinaya Mahavagga* 5

20 *Udana* i.10

21 *Samyutta-Nikaya* i.179

22 *Therigatha* 63; *Dhammapada commentary* (The Pali Text Society's *Buddhist Legends*) 8.13

23 *Digha-Nikaya* 11

24 *Udana* viii.7; *Theragatha* 260

25 *Vinaya Mahavagga* 8

26 *Anguttara-Nikaya* iv.216–20; *Sutta Nipata Commentary* i.217–4. See also the *Dictionary of Pali Proper Names*, i.291–2

27 *Vinaya Cullavagga* 5

28 *Anguttara-Nikaya* iv.192–9

29 *Digha-Nikaya* 2

30 *Anguttara-Nikaya* iv.212–6

31 *Digha-Nikaya* 16

32 *Digha-Nikaya* 16

GLOSSARY

of some terms from the Dhammapada verses

Going for Refuge

This is the way Buddhists speak of committing themselves to the spiritual path rather than worldly goals.

The Three Refuges

These are the Buddha: the ideal of wisdom and compassion embodied in the historical Buddha, but potential in all beings; the Dharma: the Truth, and the path leading to Buddhahood; the Sangha: the fellowship of those who have attained the wisdom and compassion of the Buddha and who serve as guides and inspiration to all who follow the Buddhist path.

The Four Ariyan Truths

Ariyan is an ancient Indian word meaning 'noble', and within Buddhism came to denote an expression of the highest spiritual development. They are: the truth of suffering; its cause, which is craving; the cessation of suffering; and the 'noble eightfold path' leading to the cessation of suffering.

Nirvana

The state attained by an Enlightened being. It is said to be beyond words and concepts. It is a state free from greed, hatred, and ignorance. In positive terms, it is a state imbued with a wisdom that sees into the very heart of existence and with boundless compassion. Traditional epithets for Nirvana include 'the cool cave', 'liberation', 'the island amidst the floods', 'the transcendental', and 'the further shore'

Suffering, impermanence, and insubstantiality

These are the three marks or characteristics of 'conditioned existence', which is the world of everyday phenomena, sometimes called samsara. It is called 'conditioned existence' because the Buddha saw that all phenomena constantly arise and fall away in dependence on ever-changing conditions. When the Buddha taught that conditioned existence is suffering, or unsatisfactory, he was not saying there is no happiness or pleasure to be found in everyday life, but was simply pointing out that we build our happiness on things that do not last, and therefore we suffer. True happiness is to be found only in the attainment of Enlightenment, a profound knowing and seeing of things as they really are, inseparable from ultimate wisdom and compassion.

Unskilful and Skilful

Within Buddhist ethics, these are terms used to define behaviour. Skilful actions are those motivated by mental states of tranquillity, love, and wisdom, which lead to happiness for ourselves and others. Unskilful actions are those motivated by mental states of greed, hatred, and delusion and lead to suffering for ourselves and others.

FURTHER READING

The Pali Canon

Bhikkhu Nanamoli, *The Life of the Buddha*, Buddhist Publication Society, Kandy 1978. An anthology of stories and teachings from the Pali Canon, with a commentary, compiled by Bhikkhu Nanamoli, an English Buddhist monk. An excellent introduction to the Pali Canon.

Modern translations include

Maurice Walshe, *The Long Discourses of the Buddha (Digha-Nikaya)* Wisdom Publications, Boston 1995

Bhikkhu Nanamoli and Bhikkhu Bodhi, *The Middle Length Discourses of The Buddha (Majjhima-Nikaya)*, Wisdom Publications, Boston 1995

John D. Ireland, *The Udana and the Itivuttaka*, Buddhist Publication Society, Kandy 1997

Nyanaponika Thera and Hellmuth Hecker, *Great Disciples of the Buddha*, Wisdom Publications, Boston 1997

INDEX OF PROPER NAMES